T0103530

THE SON ROSE
FROM THE WEST

THE SON ROSE FROM THE WEST

DEVI RAGHUVANSHI

PARTRIDGE

To order additional copies of this book, contact
Partridge India
000 800 10062 62
orders.india@partridgepublishing.com

www.partridgepublishing.com/india

DEDICATION

Dedicated to my Parents, who made me to read and write, while they were just the farmers.

This book is also dedicated to those who either have PhD in Romance or who are standing at the parapet to jump or plunge in LOVE.

ACKNOWLEDGEMENTS

I acknowledge and express my gratitude to my wife SUSHMA, for the input, spell check and all the inspiration and ideas, I conceived watching the degree of her patience.

My elder daughter PREETI deserves special mention for the emotional and financial support in bringing out the publication of this book.

I would like PAYAL, my younger daughter to be a partner in my this endeavour. Frankly speaking I have copied some of her blogs to make my book rich and true.

Finally I thank all my friends on Facebook, my college mates, for encouraging me to write this book. My heartfelt thanks, will not be complete unless I mentioned the big help I got from "Bhagvad Gita' and 'Google', the boss for anything.

You all are part of my these efforts BIG or SMALL.

DECLARATION

The contents of this book are wild imaginations of the author. Any resemblance of names, places or incidences are purely coincidental and unintentional.

The author does not take any responsibility for the loss or damage to anyone on account of publication of this book except he expresses his regrets for the damage if any.

DEVI RAGHUVANSHI

CHAPTER – 1

The Story begins

The story begins from a dusty village some 10 Kms away from Mathura. The village has been away for quite some time from Civilization. Almost all communities like Brahmins, members of schedule caste and tribes were staying like a homogeneous family. The Jats were the dominating community because of numbers and also because of their inherent quality of being good fighters. They only loved their land and motherland. Another community was a considerable presence of Muslims who were like a service community, mostly as brass band players for marriages or functions or the weavers for durries, carpets or bed sheets. The Jats were prosperous as they had land and at least one member was working as a teacher or at least one member from the family was in Indian Armed Forces.

Normally these Jats were very simple harmless people but they can't take anything wrong in their system or in their way. That's the reason, people call them JAT (Just Adore them) or JAT (Just Avoid Them). The story revolves around Santosh and Shehzadi, two women from different culture, different families and different communities but the definition of true friendship can only be defined by the relationship, they shared. There was not even a day, they didn't meet. There was not even one day, when Shehzadi was not offered butter milk from Santosh's kitchen. Santosh was a farmer's wife with lot of Buffaloes and Cows so milk was available in abundance. Shehzadi was a poor Muslim lady with two sons, Akbar and Anwar. She had lost her husband quite some time back. Her source of survival was her two sons working for Santosh. The elder one, Akbar was helping Karan Veer Singh for agriculture work and younger son, Anwar was employed to graze the cattle. Both the boys were actually minors but during those years, no body used to understand and follow labour laws. Santosh had five kids and one of them was, Aditya who was of same age as Anwar. Both Santosh and Karan Veer used to love their children and also were very kind and considerate to both Akbar and Anwar. They didn't have any difference between their children and Shehzadi's children. They were pure vegetarians whereas Shehzadi had few chickens so eggs and chicken mutton was cooked sometimes. Aditya was very close to Shehzadi also and used to spend lot of time with her as her kids used to be out of her house, so Shehzadi used to love and take care of Aditya like her own son. Aditya was born different. He was a breach baby. Some of his habits were unique, nobody taught him anything about these habits.

It was a common practice in the entire village that Sweeper or Sweepress used to clean the entire village and used to carry the shit on their heads to be thrown away from the houses and in the evening he or she used to visit all houses to get one Roti (Bread) from each house, they used to eat these Rotis and surplus was the food for their Pigs. Aditya used to wait till that Sweepress came, checked all the Rotis physically from the basket and then gave Roti from his house to her. Santosh used to scold him every day for having touched all the Rotis but he did not miss it even for one day. It could have been God's gift to him not to feel any difference between him and the Sweepress. He was unique since beginning.

By remaining with Shehzadi, he learnt Namaz and its Urdu verses and even the way the Muslims offer prayers. Not that he was not knowing Hindu religious epics, he was equally devoted and confident in reciting all prayers. The people in and around his village knew about it and almost everybody loved him.

CHAPTER - 2

One day, Aditya asked his father Karan Veer why Anwar is not going to school like I go. He was told by his father that it's because of financial constraints, Shehzadi could not afford his education. Aditya was different since birth. He asked a simple question, Papa we are five brothers and sisters, let's assume, we are six and treat Anwar as our brother only.

His father was taken back to shock and to a thought that his son is not a normal kid. He is either an incarnation of some Gods or God only made him so kind and generous. He thought to himself that he would surely do something for Anwar as it was a call from God and Aditya is only the media. He told Aditya that from today, Anwar is your second brother but now don't bring us your third or fourth brother and sister as I will not be able to afford it. Ok Papa, Anwar is our last brother.

Karan Veer soon realized that quality and access of education was the major concern for Anwar in that rural school as there were fewer committed teachers and also lack of proper text books and learning material. He thought for a moment and decided that he would admit Anwar also in the private school where his own kids were studying. The majority of people living in that village, had understood the importance of education and knew that this was the only way to get rid of poverty. Though this was expensive than government schools for education but he always believed that if he had to do anything, it had to be the best possible. Three pairs of school uniform, white shirt, dark grey half pent, white socks, black shoes and red tie were arranged for him. Normally the kids of Muslim parents are good looking so Anwar in school uniform, was looking like any convent or English medium school students. He was admitted in Ist Standard. Aditya by that time was in 4th Standard in the same school. He was very happy to see Anwar going to school. Age wise, Anwar was the eldest in his class as he joined school at an advance age.

The happiest man in the family after Aditya was Karan Veer as for him, educating a child like Anwar was a step towards development of a poor friendly family and finally our country. Anwar was explained about vocational skills along with its syllabus. He was also explained by Aditya to develop his interest in computer related activities. Santosh & Shehzadi thanked Aditya and Karan Veer for their noble thought and action. Everyone in the village, be it be he or she, Hindu or Muslim supported their move for Anwar whole heartedly. Aditya was different unlike any other normal kid. He was special. He was born different.

CHAPTER – 3

Anwar in two years

Anwar was sharp but raw in the beginning so apart from teaching him, his regular syllabus subjects, the modern language aptitude test was developed to teach him English language in a given span of time and under given conditions. On insistence from Aditya, Karan Veer arranged extra tutor to reduce the gap of those 4 or 5 years which were denied to him in his early childhood days. Equal stress was laid on Mathematics and Science and Anwar's transformation was bearing fruits. Soon he started conversing in English. Aditya issued specific instructions to him to talk to him in English only.

As time doesn't wait for anybody or anything, Anwar was promoted to 6th Standard, 7th Standard, 8th Standard and 9th Standard. Now there was gap of only one year between Aditya and Anwar. Aditya was preparing for his board examination of 10th Standard. Now the bond between Aditya and Anwar changed to two thick friends who couldn't stay away from each other. For Aditya, Anwar was his younger kid brother and a friend. He used to guide him in all areas including studies along with his own studies. He always used to quote Colin Powell's advice to Anwar,

"A dream doesn't become a reality through magic. It takes sweat, determination and hard work." I follow this and you will also follow the same Anwar, Aditya told him. Truly Aditya was born special.

Anwar as a true disciple, asked Aditya, who is the real winner? Or how do we define a winner? Aditya replied Anwar, "The real winners in life are the people who look at every situation with an expectation that they can make it work or make it better. A winner is someone, Anwar, who recognizes his God given talent, works his tail off to develop them into skills and uses them to accomplish his goals. Anwar, since you have both of them, so you have increased the level of my expectations. It's not like, I am giving you some high end lectures like political leaders but I will lead you by example. I have dream for you and I don't appreciate failures. We both have to prove our worth to respect the supreme sacrifice of our father who toils throughout the day in that scorching heat in paddy fields to provide us all we need. I will do it Aditya, I will do it for him, for you and for our two mothers.

Aditya made a chart for him and Anwar and pasted in front of his study area which read that **ALWAYS RESPECT**;

1) The value of Time
2) The success of Perseverance
3) The dignity of Simplicity
4) The worth of Character
5) The power of Kindness
6) The wisdom of Economy
7) The virtue of Patience

8) The improvement of Talent
9) The respect for both Mothers
10) Touching feet of Karan Veer every day morning

Yes, Aditya was born different and special.

CHAPTER – 4

Aditya & Anwar in Religious Contest

Aditya was in 10th and Anwar in 9th both studying in Junior College in their own village in the same private school. To unite India and to inject a feeling of peace, brotherhood, Govt. of India, conducted an open debate competition on all India basis for all schools, colleges and universities. The topic given to them was 'Humanity is the ultimate religion'. Thousands of students from all over India, male or female participated in this contest. The interesting part was that Anwar spoke on GITA and Aditya on QURAN.

Anwar in his opening address said, "I have been brought up in a Muslim and Hindu family and our families believe that one needs to respect and accept all religions. No religion preaches hatred. I have always been inquisitive about religion. I have read and learnt Gita from my extended family. The Gita, believed to be the divine advice of Lord Krishna, is a 700 verse Hindu scriptures. Religion unites and not divides. Anwar said that preachings of Gita written by A.C. Bhaktivedanta Swami Prabhupada, will make the world a place to live in Harmony. Gita is nobody's private property. It belongs to all irrespective of any caste, creed or religion.

When asked by the reporters of various news channels how being a Muslim, he knew so much about Gita, he promptly replied and advised all present, not to call him Muslim boy to contest Bhagvad Gita. The most important teaching that has stayed with him after reading Gita is that "you should always do the right thing and have a right faith." "I believe that there is one God but we call him in different names. My mother has taught me that in order to break free from religious discrimination, it is important for us to have an understanding of all religions and be sensitive towards them."

Anwar translated and answered 97.5% questions and verses of Gita. He specifically mentioned Aditya's name who changed his perception of life and now he feels that he is above religion. He is now a human rather than a Muslim like Aditya is a human than a Hindu.

Aditya while expressing his faith said that there are many similarities between Hinduism and Islam. For example, Jihad is same in both the religions. Jihad is an Arabic word which means to strive or to struggle like if a student strives to pass an examination, he or she is doing Jihad. Jihad is only one of the forms of fighting which is always against evils and is common for both Hindus and Muslims.

The theme of self sacrifice for God and humanity is common in both the Gita and the Quran. Both the epics, the text gives a directive to fight against;

1) Oppression and injustice
2) Against non-believers who refuse to believe

Minor contradictions should not make this world a hell to live. The biggest religion according to Aditya is Humanity. I have a brother Anwar. We have brought him up as a Muslim but he at times proves to be better Hindu than all of us.

Both Anwar and Aditya won the contest in their respective categories from 6000 participants. Yes, Aditya was born different and he was special.

CHAPTER – 5

Aditya under counselling

Aditya like most of the students completing their 10th Standard, was confused about deciding a right career path. For a successful career, careful planning and following it up with a workable plan was needed. Since there was no defined advice from his father, so for deciding a potential career, Aditya attended educational fairs, career guidance seminars with several colleges and he was able to reach to a path of career exploration decision making ability.

To obtain a strong foundation for further studies like graduation or post-graduation, a good option, he considered was to opt for 10+2 with Science stream with mathematics and computer. He was briefed by the counselors that this combination of Science and Maths would offer him lucrative career options after 12th Standard. This would open a way for Engineering. He would be required to concentrate on Physics, Chemistry, Mathematics, Computer Science and English language. He was also briefed about various coaching classes in Kota and Delhi which helped students to prepare for Engineering College admissions like IITs, NITs, BITs etc. Since there was no financial constraints for Aditya, he made up his mind to go for Engineering and to follow the road map given to him by his advisors. His father Karan Veer agreed to support his son whatever option he would go in for. With these thoughts and guidelines, Aditya took admission in 11th Science in Govt. Higher Secondary College, Mathura.

Since the college was 10 miles away from Aditya's village, so it was not possible to travel this distance every day, so he became a hosteller and used to visit his parents on weekends. He was basically from a rural background and parents were not much educated but he still chose his career path entirely at his own efforts. Yes, Aditya was born different and he was special.

CHAPTER – 6

Aditya in Hostel in 11th & 12th

Aditya spent two years in Govt. College Hostel. He not only studied his subjects but also studied the behavioural changes in his fellow hostellers. While he concentrated on his basic aim of studies like Arjun's bow on fish eye of Mahabharat, many students used their stay in hostel as an opportunity to have fun including drinking, smoking, going out for clubs and movies. His friends used to make joke or pass sarcastic comments like Aditya is a spiritual guru and finally join Patanjali in search of those medicinal herbs and his basic aim of becoming an engineer, will end up in Haridwar jungles.

Aditya mastered his knowledge in Physics, Chemistry, Mathematics and English language. Unbelievably, he completed all required subjects of 11th & 12th in Eleventh only and Twelveth was only a revision and repetition only while he was preparing for his 11th final exams, he ensured that Anwar was just following his footsteps. Aditya passed 11th securing first rank in his class, Anwar stood 16th in 10th board exam of U.P. Board where 12 Lac students appeared. He was very happy for his kid brother and brought him also in the same Govt. College in 11th Standards with same subjects. Time flew, seasons changed and Aditya appeared for his 12th board exams and passed in Ist division securing distinction in Physics, Chemistry, Maths and Computer Science. He was ranked 21st in the entire state of U.P.

After passing out 12th he also joined coaching class at Kota Rajasthan for IIT admission. As his efforts and luck favoured, he was selected in IIT Roorkee in B.Tech Computer Science. Aditya before joining at IIT Roorkee had one month's time which he utilized in shaping Anwar to a professionally oriented student. He thought it be most wanting because Anwar was in 12th Standard in same college and same hostel. Since Aditya had an experience of hostel life when he saw all good and bad of life, he just wrote a small description on hostel life for his kid brother.

"Life in a hostel is fun but it is a roller coaster ride too.

1) MESS - Mess is actually a mess. Do not expect four homemade meals. You will get only Potatoes in place of vegetables. It is a national vegetable in hostel.

2) MAGGI - You will survive on Maggi because it was a life line for me and would be for you. It was so important for everyone out there that it invariably became like our birthday cake.

3) CHAI - Aditya became a Chai-holic. Tea was way of life and he became such a tea lover that he knew locations of all different Chai Taparis/ Tea joints at every corner around his hostel.

4) PARTY in HOSTEL - It was like hostel anthem. Desi Bollywood music at high volumes, disturbed

everybody but who cares really? The hostellers never needed any particular reason to party.

5) SLEEP - In a hostel, you are a victim of Insomnia. There are so much of hyper activities that a peaceful sleep is either a dream or luxury. Aditya used to come home on Saturdays and Sundays to steal few good winks. Nights were fun in hostel when you gossip, play games and party.

6) PHILOSOPHER - The advice on any subject from your fellow hostellers is free and in abundance so you land up becoming a Philosopher. The advice varies from Lovelorn people to broken hearts.

7) STUDIES - It was and is a fashion to study just before examinations like engineers but Aditya remained an exceptional case.

8) MANAGE EXPENSES – This is one of the best achievement and Aditya learnt the real value of money and the ways to manage every expense on the source available to him.

9) LOVE & AFFECTION – Since Aditya was away from the home, he felt and developed an increased love and affection to home, sweet home.

10) RESPONSIBILITY – The hostel life teaches you to become independent and more responsible. You get up early by your own, wash your utensils and clothes. There are many things, that you learn at home, school and college but true learning experience comes from leading a hostel life."

11) Anwar, you will naturally gain a sense of independence and responsibility. If you still need anything more, Aditya is just a phone call away.

Your aim is defined and to pursue, it will be your Gita, Quran or Bible. Just be a human. Anwar heard and read everything and his eye contact with Aditya, assured Aditya for everything for times to come.

Aditya was born different. He was special.

CHAPTER – 7

Aditya in IIT Roorkee

Before going to Roorkee, Aditya spent a good time with all his friends of the village with whom he spent his childhood days and they all recollected their old memories, like playing Gilli-Danda, climbing on Mango & Jamun trees, swimming in canal. Aditya and Anwar were so closely knit that all their friends used to comment on Aditya "Amar, Akbar and Anthony but where is Anthony? Aditya jovially used to tell them, "wait, I will have Anthony also. Wait for some time and you all will proudly say, "Amar, Akbar, Anthony."

There were some sarcastic comments from few friends and villagers that Aditya, you have become MAHAAN (great) by educating Anwar and probably making him a big man but what about AKBAR? He still remains where he was when his father died. Still burning his fat in the same scorching heat in your fields. Aditya replied, "Even my father is doing the same thing under same adverse ambient conditions but I will ensure that at some point of time in his life, I will make him owner of some of the land where he will be doing his farming independently.

Yes, Aditya was born different. He was special.

CHAPTER – 8

Santosh & Shehzadi in conversation

Shehzadi once casually mentioned to Santosh that you have been doing a lot of favours to me and Anwar. Nobody does it in present days and even you have lot of responsibilities to perform. I can work at different places and arrange for Anwar's education. Santosh got wild and told Shehzadi that she would not let Shehzadi become a great woman by people appreciating all the time that Shehzadi worked hard as a maid for cleaning and sweeping other's homes to arrange for her son's education as Santosh would only be doing all arrangements. My son, Aditya wants it and it is final once for all.

Shehzadi became emotional and told Santosh that her husband didn't die a natural death but he was poisoned by that radical tailor Juman. My husband was a human first and Muslim later. His this attitude didn't go well with him. My husband told me this before dying. He said, "Don't reveal it to anybody otherwise Juman's entire family would be wiped out. Tell my sons once they grow up and understand, let them not have any feeling of revenge." Why you didn't tell me this? I was your best friend. I didn't tell you because of this only. Shehzadi was not educated but she said, "Be soft. Do not let the world make you hard. Do not let pain, make you hate. Do not let the bitterness steal your sweetness. You are very kind Shehzadi. I would have made Juman's life a living hell. Do not bother about your sons. For Aditya, they are like real brothers and even you have spoilt Aditya by feeding him chicken and eggs. We are pure vegetarians. Aditya can recite almost all Quran verses and he is a real human being and part of it goes due to your love to him. Yes, Aditya was born different. He is special.

CHAPTER – 9

Floods damage Ankur

Ankur, an orphanage children home is situated in the low lying area of IIT Roorkee. It was a Sunday when Aditya and his hostel mates were waiting for tanker water supply for taking bath etc. There was tremendous heat and water supply was at its critical mode. There was no proper water even for drinking. Some miracle happened. It started raining, dark clouds with thunders covered the entire area and the intensity of rains increased. It was a pleasure to see rains in the parched region of Roorkee but what happened subsequently, was that rains became a fury. IIT measured the heavy rainfall which was 375% more than the benchmark rainfall during a normal monsoon. Soon the streets of Roorkee, became rivers and low lying areas got submerged into 6 feet to 8 feet water. The heavy rains resulted in large flash floods and massive landslides. The continuous rains in Uttarakhand resulted excess water on the streets of Roorkee.

The most affected area was the low lying area close to IIT campus which housed Ankur. There were close to 100 girls from 4 years to 17 years. Normally the Ankur orphanage is supported by outside donations and help from churches. The water entered in the orphanage damaging all stored food supplies, kitchen and prayer room. The place was cut off from rest of the city, leaving the inhabitants stranded inside with panic and cries by girls for rescue. What a deluge? Aditya with his five friends gathered courage and ventured out forming the chain of 5 persons and reached Ankur. Seeing these boys, the girls had a little solace and agreed to come out with Aditya in the same way of forming human chain. Jane was the eldest of all and she could know Aditya and team as she was also a student of B.Sc.(IT) in same IIT. She did have a fear of her safety and also safety of other girls because of these young boys but since there was no option and sister Nancy was with them. She accompanied the boys and they all were brought to Hostel No.1 dining room. Aditya managed the permission and all arrangements of food and stay for everyone till the situation improved. He also collected a donation of Rupees Two Lacs from all his friends and hostel-mates to meet emergency expenses for all affected.

Jane was watching all this and was slowly generating a trust in the man. She did talk to sister Nancy who also had a similar opinion about Aditya. Jane thought to herself that Aditya was a gentleman dude. Aditya by nature was an explorer and whatever came to his mind, he had a habit of reaching to the root of its existence. He found Jane also a bit special and he asked Jane, her background. Jane wanted to know why Aditya was entering into her private life? Aditya saw her actions and reactions during crisis so he simply told Jane, "You are a super woman. You laugh even if sometimes, you are sad. You are loving and giving, even if sometimes, you are exhausted. Your motto that appears to me is what doesn't kill us, makes us stronger. You never give up and learn from your mistakes which make you an incredibly strong woman and your biggest realization is "BE YOURSELF".

It all started on a casual chat but Jane took his views genuinely and soon Jane's thought of Aditya's sympathy, turned into mutual trust and mutual respect. Jane promised Aditya to share her past and to know more of Aditya. Till now Aditya only had a soft corner for Jane and a desire to meet her more often. They both had a divine relationship. Aditya was born different and he was special.

CHAPTER – 10

Aditya wants to know

Jane trusted Aditya like death so when Aditya asked her background, Jane said, that Aditya, when I look at your face, I see a Jesus, I see a Krishna of childhood and I naturally start trusting my instincts. I don't know Aditya but for me, you are mild benign, benignant and compassionate. She starts narrating her story. She only remembers her life when she was brought to Ankur by her mother. She was only three years old then. After her mother left her, she never came back to Ankur. What could be reasons or compulsions, she is not aware of.

The Ankur is an orphanage managed by Christian sisters who provide food, shelter and education to the children who had lost their parents or whose parents can't afford basic requirement like food. The kids also were from the poor families where their mothers are working as domestic help and the fathers are drunkards. The entire set up of Ankur, is managed on donations from well to do families or Churches. She continued that the Sister of the orphanage cared for me as if she was the mother. She was probably the most loving, the most kindest person I have ever met. I grew up to 8 years and was put up as incharge of small kids and I treated them just the way, they treated me.

For months and years, I never recalled the incident of my mother leaving me there. I had a mental void for the entire month following her departure. Flashes would sometimes pop into my memory and then the time sort of leaps forward. I once asked sister Nancy why my mother left me here? When you grow up, I will not hide anything from you Jane, sister Nancy replied. I went to school. It was sad at times and depressing but I just healed and moved on. I reached Standard 10th. Apart from the hard work of studies, I had some horrible struggle and I had to fight the demon. The person who sponsored my education since Ist Standard, came to meet me in Ankur. He normally was a visitor like any other donor so his meeting me, didn't raise any suspicion. Since everyone was away for evening prayers, he took advantage of the situation and he pulled me and kissed me. For the first time, I tasted the dirty smell of that human body and a feeling of being an orphan. I cried a lot more than that when my mother left me and quickly discovered that tears have very little purpose. I lost the entire strength of body and mind and fell straight in sister Nancy's lap. Oh my God, what a nightmare, I passed through.

It was when sister Nancy played my mother, my sister, how she made me feel. My life was on right track and doing well for myself. My mind digested that incident and I recovered from it and haven't suffered for it more than the minimum expected. I miss my mother a great deal and would love to talk with her. It was the most surreal feeling being 15 years old only.

From that day onwards as much as I acted independent and did everything for myself. I couldn't leave Ankur. I was a kid who didn't know what will happen next. I have to grow up fast. This experience has taught me, to fully rely on myself at this age. Sometimes when people talk about their parents, I reach to a vacuum of speech but it's like that I have to live with it. In next two years, I completed my 12th Standard and stood first in the Science group and also in entire St. Stephen's Junior College. Sister Nancy was God's gift to me. She sacrificed everything for me and today, the radiance I saw on her face because of my success, cannot be described in words but could be felt within. Thank God, Thank Sister Nancy, Thanks Ankur for a safe shelter.

CHAPTER - 11

Aditya experiences life at IIT Roorkee

From the beginning of Ist year Engineering, Aditya was mesmerised by the beauty of campus. His college was the oldest in India which was converted into IIT. As usual he worked hard on his studies and passed Ist year of Engineering very comfortably and respectfully. After passing out, he felt that this was the most amazing and satisfactory day of his life, however the journey was long and his courage to face situations was longer.

At the same time, Anwar also passed his 12th Standard. He went to Karan Veer and Karan Veer asked him how many marks you got more than Aditya? Anwar hesitantly told him, five. He asked Karan Veer, "Uncle, please get me admitted in B.Sc. I will do B.Sc., B.Ed. and start teaching. Why not what Aditya was doing? Engineering is very expensive and the expenditure for both Aditya & me, would be too much so I thought, I would study in Mathura. What would Aditya think of his father if I accepted your request? You knew Aditya very well? You are Aditya's brother and my second son. Are you aware of this or forgotten? I remember it Papa but this is going to be too much. I am not sure how would I repay your debt? Karan Veer then told him, "It is easy to pay. You also get another Anwar or Aditya and own the responsibility similar to what I and Aditya are doing." Trust me Papa, I would always remember your these words, said Anwar."

He appeared in combined entrance test CET and got admission in IIT, MUMBAI. Karan Veer made all arrangements for him to join Engineering at MUMBAI. Aditya came all the way from Roorkee to make his kid brother comfortable in college and hostel in MUMBAI.

Aditya while studying in IIT Roorkee, made a specific observation about the life of a student in IIT Roorkee, specially if he or she is hosteller. He wrote like this "The life in Engineering College specially when you are staying in a hostel of campus, is real fun to have in one's entire lifetime. Some of the facts and figures preserved on moments are unique which are not found in any other institutions. You may be having any syllabus, any branch, the preparation for exams starts a night before the exam. Your normal day starts at 10-11am and week stays for 5 days. Saturday and Sunday are actually to recover lost sleep. In hostels, birthdays are real fun to celebrate with loud music on Bollywood songs. Classes are meant to recover the sleepless nights. You are a hero if you have a girl around you. Bunking the classes and hanging around medical college for bird watching is a habit. Industrial visits and educational trips are picnic days.

This was the CMP (Common Minimum Programme) to be followed by absolute majority of Engineering students excluding the minority which consisted people like Aditya.

Another incident which happened in Aditya's life would also need mention. Aditya was not only a very sincere and intelligent student, he was the best athlete. His established records of 100m run, 110m hurdle, high jump, long jump and hop step and jump, recorded in all IIT athletic meets and they have not been broken till today. In the process of attending these events and practice, he had to miss some of his classes and practicals which didn't go well with his head of department HOD. He called Aditya one day in his chamber and told him, "Aditya, I know, you are a good athlete but this is not going to help you in your career so you will have to choose one of them either athletics or regular studies." The message was loud and clear and Aditya had no option but to leave his sports activities though it was quite painful for him because he was the standard in all athletic events.

Time flew, seasons changed and Aditya reached in 3rd year of Engineering. Based on his experience, he sent a small note in form of an Email to his younger brother Anwar which was like an advice to him "Don't lose hope, Don't give up. Life is a marathon not a sprint. What really matters is not winning small events in life but not giving up after heavy setbacks. It is better to avoid them but if you have unfortunately hit the bottom then what matters is how you get up and bounce back and if you can bounce back then there is nothing in the world that you will fear. Stop complaining, stop whining, take charge." Anwar, you are a wonder boy. Keep it up. Aditya was born different, he was special.

CHAPTER – 12

Aditya falls for Jane

Many people say that there is nothing called love at first sight and it doesn't exist. But truth is, love at first sight can happen to anyone, anytime, anyplace and anywhere. Aditya first got attracted to Jane and basically it was physical attraction however this attraction was beyond sexual desire. When asked by Jane why he had fallen for her, his reply was that Jane, your eyes were the window to your soul to me. Your eyes were just the sample of your incredible qualities, both within and out. Your eyes captivated me in my first meeting with you in Ankur and I always wanted to know you from that moment. Jane was taken aback. She thought for a moment and said, yes, there was something about you Aditya, that just resonated with me. "You are very genuine and unbelievably sweet."

Their meetings increased and so the feelings for each other. Since Aditya was born different and he was special so their puppy love survived the ravages of time, physical needs and mistakes of impulsive love. In case of Jane, it revealed the way the woman was developing a much stronger sense of self in many spaces not traditionally defined as Feminist but certainly marked by mobility and self-realization. For her, this was no longer a world in which most women would simply vote for whomever their husbands tell them to or rely on men to form their individual views and personality. Jane was a beauty with brains. When Jane saw Aditya, the first time, she liked him and wanted to know him but he was a very shy guy and was mostly a silent serious and preoccupied and would only speak on subject but when he opened up and she knew him, then loving him was a blessing.

CHAPTER – 13

Anwar follows Aditya

Anwar was not only following Aditya in studies but also in the field which was written by destiny and guided by cupid. Honestly he had no intentions of following in love. It was very natural and all of a sudden. He was hardly acquainted with the concept of "Love at first sight". It all started when Anwar saw Anandita in the carpentry workshop. She was struggling with the wooden plainer to make a sample piece work assigned by the carpentry instructor in the first year of Engineering. The sweat, then the brisk smile on her face and those bewitching eyes, blew his senses away completely. For Anwar, it was not completely her beauty that mesmerised him but something unique in her which Anwar couldn't describe. Anandita, it appears to Anwar, came from a typical rich Rajput family from Udaipur. She had that personality to define her origin. She was 5 feet 7 inches fair complexion, big dark eyes with long eye laces, slightly curl long hair till waist line fully covered with that Salwar Kameez. There was no conversation except few eye contacts and mutual smile exchanges out of courtesy but Anwar felt the impact and some rush of blood in his nerves. Anwar offered her help in carpentry but the demonstrator ensured that this link is not connected between them.

He met Anandita for the second time during a cultural festival of IIT MUMBAI, inter Branch competitions. She was representing Computer Science branch and Anwar, the Mechanical one. There was an instant spark. Anandita introduced herself first, "I am Anandita Singh, Ist B.Tech Computer Science. I am Anwar Shaikh, Ist B.Tech, Mechanical Engineering. After hearing his name, she had a first jerk reaction of him being a Muslim but composed herself and said I have come from Rajasthan quota. I am from U.P. quota and belong to Mathura." They both spent approx. 2 hours more or less like strangers except there were exchange of greetings. Anwar basically was a bit reserved type, self-occupied and also a little introvert whereas Anandita was frank outspoken and easy to start conversation. The biggest asset, Anwar had was that he was the most handsome guy around like a typical Pathan, capable of generating attention from any female friends.

Anwar was so good looking that all his batch mates wanted to be good friends to him but the way he conducted himself, the girls were not sure of, the way to approach him so all gathered and put the onus on Anandita to ensure that he opens up. Anandita sent him a mail pretending to be his girlfriend and asked him to meet in the college canteen. Anwar was sure of facing a prank from some of his friends so he confirmed of his meeting her with a remark of "I love you too". The mail ID was fake but he made it to the canteen where he didn't find any girl. All he saw in the canteen was one of the ugliest Tanzanian girl. The moment, he wanted to leave the canteen, the entire group appeared from nowhere and started laughing loud. He started blushing in front of them. Every female was there except Anandita whom he expected to be there for sure.

Anwar was studying heat engines in his hostel room one day when someone knocked at his door and came inside smiling and said, "today you have a bad day. Be ready to be slapped any moment but as everything happens for a reason, he noticed Anandita coming to meet him." The casual conversation started with an intent to know each other. She confessed that she was instigated by her friends to play some pranks on you as you were conceived to be reserved and curtained with some insulation from all her female college mates.

Anwar knew for sure even Anandita also knew for sure that neither it was going to affect her or his life nor they were going to achieve any personal satisfaction or fun out of it but Anwar that day felt that Anandita was the prettiest of all and special like his brother Aditya. The desire to meet and the desire to speak to each other increased since that day.

Out for a stroll one evening, Anwar saw her heading towards the hostel gate in a rickshaw, he couldn't resist asking here where did she go every day at same time? To the old age home for one hour daily to talk to those old people who had nobody to talk. My mom had advised me to do it religiously everyday as they didn't need anything except your time. I have been doing it from last one year. This gesture from Anandita aroused huge respect in his eyes and he asked Anandita whether he could also come along with her? Anandita agreed to take him along for a noble cause.

CHAPTER – 14

Aditya visits Jaisalmer Rajasthan

Aditya had a friend Aftab from Rajasthan, his classmate who lost his father in a communal clash. He had to go to his native place in Jaisalmer district. Aditya accompanied him to console his family. To his surprise, he saw a group of women clad in black clothes who according to a custom in that area of Rajasthan, were hired as professional mourner after the death of a male relative of the family. These women are called Rudaalis.

They were publicly expressing the grief of the family members who are not permitted to display emotions due to social status. The impact of their mourning also compels other people at the funeral to cry. Aditya wondered that those kind of traditions were still kept up by the rich people. Aditya felt bad for this breed of women who earned their livelihood by professional mourning. He made up his mind to do something for this community once he settled down in life. Yes, Aditya was born different. He was special.

CHAPTER – 15

Aditya completes Engineering

Aditya never seemed to manage to finish all his work. How times flies! Days, months and years crept by and he was finding himself preparing for his final year engineering exams. So far Aditya was only writing exams and pass but in final year, he had project work also. His project work was designing air-conditioning chillers with an efficiency of 95 percent suitable as per green building norms which required his lot of time to learn the requisite latest technologies and also improve upon communication skills. More than anything also he needed to know how to behave professionally with others.

Aditya also had in his mind either to appear for Gate, GRE or be regularly in touch with the placement agencies. He also had to prepare himself for college campus interviews. Normally every student was depending on the placement office of the college for placement but Aditya in addition to this was browsing internet for placement offers as he was of the view to remember that it was his career so he has to be proactive. He made a list of companies which are normally coming to IIT Roorkee and studied their details of the product and their balance sheets. He finally mastered, good knowledge of the fundamentals, good communication skill and pleasing manners. Since most of the companies, generally discuss regarding project work so Aditya gained good knowledge on air-conditioning chillers, their performance and their comparative selling features.

Jane was aware of his this routine so she was constantly helping him for his preparations for campus interview. She was particularly taking interest in Aditya's personal grooming, selection of his clothes for interviews, styling his hair to cut it short. Aditya asked Jane that if he got a chance to work in multinational companies like Diakin, Toshiba, Trane, Carrier, all air-conditioning companies or alternately in Indian Army as Captain in campus interview what according to her would be the best choice? Indian Army of course! was the reply from Jane. May be financially, this choice may not be lucrative but service in Uniform, will be my choice. Aditya said, "Financially also, Indian Army is a good preposition. Many companies came and Aditya got few good options also but finally he accepted to join Indian Army as Captain in EME division."

Jane came with a bouquet of fresh flowers to congratulate him and they both decided to celebrate the occasion together. Aditya suggested to have dinner at a highway restaurant called Sher-E-Punjab which was famous for their Punjabi cuisine. Jane agreed for the place as it was known to her and promised to meet Aditya there at 8pm. Aditya picked up some nice roses and orchid bouquet and he was sure that no woman on earth hated receiving flowers. Jane came exactly at 8pm. Aditya greeted her with flowers. She knew that

Aditya was a thoughtful, generous and was having a sense of aesthetics. She loved all his old time gestures of courtesy. As a cultured dude, he opened the door, pulled chair for her.

Jane wanted a gentleman like Aditya in her life because this type of behaviour would show that Aditya had a class, good breeding, respect and a certificate that he had been raised right by his mother and the family. Aditya offered Jane, the menu card which she returned to Aditya to order. Aditya quipped, "since there is a difference in our eating habits, you being a non-vegetarian and me a vegetarian, I thought, I would give you a choice. Jane said, we will have Punjabi vegetarian food today." Aditya said, "Ok, you order Punjabi vegetarian food. I will only add one butter chicken in main course and fish tikka in the starters for you." Jane looked into Aditya's eyes straight and nodded with beautiful smile in agreement. They had nice dinner. They both discussed lot of things of college, hostel, church, clothes, hobbies but they were still away from being close to each other. Jane rode a pillion on Aditya's bike after the dinner and Aditya suggested if they could stop for a cup of hot coffee. Jane agreed as even she wanted to spend a little more time with Aditya. Aditya felt the heat or warmth of Jane's body which was touching him. Even Jane felt the same heat which remained undefined and unspoken. The only thing Aditya could utter to Jane after mustering courage was, "Jane, you have beautiful eyes and cryptic smile" though Jane expected a little more from Aditya. He dropped Jane at her place after coffee at CCD and said good night to Jane which was very lovingly reciprocated by her. She expected a tight hug from Aditya, if not a parting kiss, but as you all know, that Aditya was born different and he was special. Jane thanked him for the evening and told him that she really had fun with him and Aditya only hoped a future date. Someone had entered in his mind and occupied a small place in his human heart. He all along his way, was thinking about Jane and only Jane. After reaching hostel, Aditya sent a text message to Jane, "Today I felt like giving you a tight hug and a passionate kiss, I think we have fallen in serious love." Sharp came the reply, "who stopped you dude? You thought, "I should have done that?" Any way………….. Aditya, you are simply INNOCUOUS, Bye.

He completed his Engineering and sent his acceptance to join ARMY in September. Jane also completed her Engineering as B.Sc. IT and she joined one leading Engineering College of Roorkee in September.

CHAPTER – 16

Akbar gets married

Akbar, the elder brother of Anwar, also grew up to the marriageable age. He was promoted as a tractor and thresher driver. He also acquired significant knowledge and hands on experience in repairing tractors, motorcycles, house wiring and repairs of tubewells. Akbar became a service centre in himself and Karan Veer helped him to open a small shop and workshop for such repairs.

Now Shehzadi, Santosh and Karan Veer thought of arranging a suitable bride for Akbar. Under pressure from Badi Mummy (Santosh), he gave his consent.

Santosh had a very big social circle all over in the range of 15 Kilometers. She immediately contacted Fatima, her friend and suggested her to marry her daughter Gul to Akbar. Gul was educated and was a teacher in primary school. Gul, a, very beautiful and cultured girl, was the most suitable match for Akbar for two reasons, one Akbar was also a handsome, good looking man, a real Pathan, two, he was now established with the help of Bade Papa (Karan Veer). Fatima and her husband Anisur Rehman, were happy for Akbar, being a moderate Muslim and a good human being.

They both felt assured of a peaceful and purposeful life for both Gul and Akbar.

Aditya was in full agreement with the decision taken by all.

Nikah was conducted as the original meaning of the word 'Nikah' is the physical relationship between man and woman. It is also used secondarily to refer to the contract of marriage which makes that relationship lawful. It was expressly understood and stressed to both of them that the goal was not simply to produce any child for next generation but also to produce children who would be obedient to Allah and the parents. All the Muslim traditions were followed including MEHR (Guarantee) of Rs.50,000/- and 50 grams of Gold which was actually arranged by Karan Veer as Gul's parents and Shehzadi were all poor. Aditya as a gesture of magnanimity, made Akbar, an owner of one bigha cultivational land as he had promised his villagers and childhood friends in the past. Aditya, Anwar and the family celebrated Akbar's marriage. Aditya also arranged a flower decorated car to bring Gul to Shehzadi's place. Aditya was born different and he was special.

CHAPTER – 17

Aditya proposes Jane

Aditya joined army and was in Hyderabad for one year training. Jane also took up teaching I.T. as lecturer in a private engineering college. Even though both of them had plenty of things to do but the distance between them gave a feeling of loneliness. Loneliness is a very uncomfortable feeling which causes many people to become abnormal and bankrupt in thoughts but the very thought of meeting Jane after six months made his heart rate, blood pressure and brain wave activity decrease to acceptable levels and this happened within seconds.

Aditya called up Jane and informed her that he would be coming to Roorkee for two weeks break. He also hinted that he would have a serious discussion this time with her. No doubt, they were in constant touch with each other on Facebook, Whatsapp and Skype and used to talk dirty also sometimes to maintain the warmth of their long distance relationship.

Aditya after six months, as scheduled, came to Roorkee and met sister Nancy and asked her permission for a day out with Jane. Sister Nancy was so firmly convinced that

Jane could go out with him and there would be nothing immoral between both of them. They both went out for a picnic cum lunch in the nearby resort. Aditya by nature, was more matured than his age and so was Jane so he did not beat around the bush and told Jane that he would like to marry her. It wasn't a shock for Jane as she expected this now or a little later. She always found Aditya true to his personality and only asked Aditya, "Can we discuss it now?" Yes, said Aditya and also expressed his thoughts like, "The two people who cannot be emotionally open with each other, can never have true intimacy and love. We must learn to share our feelings with each other without being afraid of being vulnerable to fear. It will be dangerous, with the person, you intend marrying, you should have a feeling of being safe."

"To get married, you must be sure that you have a great communication. It is of prime importance to communicate when you have problem and disagreement however big or small."

Jane added, "One of the most important principles of marriage is taking care of each other's needs, wanting to give each other pleasure. We need to respect and admire the person, we marry. You have to be patient with each other and not criticize to put other person down." Aditya, I have few question to ask, "As a female, I have to understand that you are ready to take responsibility for the wife and the family. Are you Ok with it?" Yes, Jane, I am ready to take all the responsibility of you and your future family. Now I have a question for you. "Jane, as a woman, are you ready to understand that your man needs your respect and support. Yes, I am ready for." They both agreed to be husband and wife with a clear concept in their minds as spiritual compatibility was one of the best way to ensure happiness and they would both maintain their individuality in inter religion marriage. They had good lunch and dinner and Aditya dropped Jane in Ankur. Jane informed Sister Nancy who was very happy and gave Jane a cryptic smile.

CHAPTER – 18

Anwar completes his Engineering

Anwar completed his B.Tech Degree. He was offered Jobs by various companies like INTEL but he declined Job offers because he aimed at competing Administrative exams IAS. He discussed with Aditya and took up an assignment in Rao's Academy for teaching IIT aspirants and also joined as a student in the same academy for IAS preparations.

Meanwhile Anandita joined Infosys at Gurgaon. She made arrangement to stay as a paying guest in one of her relation's house. As the destiny wished both Anwar and Anandita became together in Delhi.

The regular meetings between them started developing into an affair. Anwar always liked her bold attitude towards anything including life. She always used to tell him that she was not scared of anybody except God and she loved her parents the most. Anwar used to say always, "You are a super woman. You laugh even if sometimes you are sad. You are loving and giving even if sometimes you are exhausted. Your motto is, what doesn't kill us makes us stronger. You never give up and learn from your mistakes which make you an incredibly strong woman. Your biggest realization is BE YOURSELF." She asked Anwar whether she thought of her like that? Anwar replied with an affirmative and also said that it was true in case of your dealing with others but in his case, she was always melting. "You are in a wrong impression Anwar." Always remember that men are from Mars and women from Venus. Some incidences of life are like leeches which can't be removed without being expressed.

Anandita asked Anwar right in front of his face, peeping deep into his eyes "Anwar, I only hope that you have not fallen for me"? what if I say, yes?"

Anandita -you are a Muslim completely different than what I preach and practice. I understand that your laws on marriage are different than ours so our alliance and resonance will need to be defined by you well before, we take a plunge.

Anwar -I am a born Muslim but brought up in Hindu environment. I trust Gita and respect Quran. I trust that humanity is the biggest religion. I think, I have told you that I have won the all school/college contest on Gita.

Anandita -Jokingly, Anwar, it should not happen that I continue saying those three magical words. I love you, and one morning, you tell me those three magical words TTT.

Anwar just smiled and hugged her. Anwar promised that he would offer her an abundance of miracles every day. He would have the power to banish her loneliness and would be her door way to heaven on earth.

They both went to ISKCON and prayed to almighty to give them strength to remove any temptation to judge one another and help them not to ever forget each other. They both promised to God that they would remain together in heart and mind as well as body. They would never criticize or be cruel to each other. They both wished to grow wise in relationship. They reminded themselves that they would grow in each other as the most beautiful woman and the most beautiful man for heavens to come. After this, they both had the feeling of deep, warm intimate, luxurious, spiritual experience of wild, passionate and unfettered love.

He confessed to Aditya whatever was in his destiny. Aditya needed some time to think but told Anwar not to cheat Anandita. His voice was firm and defiant. Yes, Bhai (Brother) was born different and he was special.

CHAPTER – 19

Aditya discusses Jane with Karan Veer

Aditya with so many aspirations and imaginations in his mind, went to his native village to meet his parents. He was given a hero's welcome by all young and old for his uniform status. He was invited by his school, Junior College to address the students. He was a hero and a guiding factor for everyone out there. Aditya always had an equation with his father to ask him to do anything but this time, he preferred to talk to his mother.

He met his father at the farm house. He discussed everything but Jane, his girlfriend. In the evening after dinner when Karan Veer went out to meet his friends as he always used to do, he told his mother that he had a girl, a Christian girl whom he would like to marry. Her name was Jane and was studying with her in IIT Roorkee. Santosh was taken aback as she didn't expect this from Aditya. She got the shock of her life. For a moment, she didn't react but after some time, she asked Aditya to talk to his father. She had no guts to either accept or reject Jane. She only told Aditya that his father had promised some Dhirendra Dahiya of Haryana to marry you with his daughter. Dahiya is some senior minister in Haryana Govt. and he had fixed up a meeting with him where you would also be present. It is tomorrow. But Maa, I had also committed to Jane. Jane was a beautiful girl, professionally qualified and a lecturer in engineering college. Maa, she was an orphan and one orphanage in Roorkee, had supported her from her primary education to Engineering education. Santosh said, "She is not sure of his father's reaction but even Dahiya's daughter is also very beautiful, 5 feet 6 inches tall and working as software engineer in Gurgaon. I have seen her, she is one of the best girl, I have seen for you so far. But Maa, I can't afford to accept any other alliance except Jane's so you please speak to Papa and try to make him understand."

She heard him patiently and seeing the determination she only requested Aditya not to cheat Jane as she must have already seen so much of hardship in her life and asked Aditya to show her picture at least. Aditya didn't take even one second to take it out of his purse and gave it to her mother. On one glance, Aditya could feel a sense of appreciation on his mother's face and he felt, part of exams like Semesters, he had already cleared. Now the main exam was to be cleared. He called up Jane and gave her the progress report. Santosh briefed her husband in the late night and then the volcano erupted. Karan Veer wanted to talk to Aditya urgently but Santosh asked him to defer it for tomorrow. Aditya was awake but was pretending to be in fast a sleep mode.

Dahiya family were supposed to come next day evening so everything had to be sorted out before they arrived. Aditya couldn't sleep the whole night. He was trying to analyse the situation and was afraid of the coming events tomorrow. His concepts were clear as he knew that in arranged marriage all the cards are on the table which doesn't happen in love marriage. In India, the situation is such that the parents are pressurized from the very beginning of their parenthood from their peers and relatives about status or honour and other irrelevant stuff which get prioritize on love and care. Indian parents specially from Western India find it difficult to digest the fact that their children are capable of choosing their own life partners. India is a vast country with so many religions, castes and languages and every caste has so many sub-castes with its unique dialect, food habits customs, rituals etc. The main problem is every sect of people including his father, don't want change. That's why Indian parents are so manipulative while marrying off their kids, treat love marriage as some kind of domestic rebel. Aditya was trying to find solutions of all these situations and in the process, when he slept? he didn't know.

Karan Veer called Aditya during breakfast and wanted to hear him out directly. Aditya honestly confessed that he was deeply in love with Jane deeply and he couldn't think of any other options. His father asked him whether he was taking this decision under any pressure? Was he in actual deep love or was that only a temporary infatuation? Karan Veer assured his son that he would get a more beautiful girl than Jane, more qualified. Aditya told his father, "You know me Papa. I don't take decisions without thinking with a balanced mind. I am your son and normally I take matured decisions." Papa, I can't remain without Jane. Karan Veer placed too many arguments to convince him but nothing helped. He also knew that Aditya was never so firm and defiant so he would be correct. We would discuss this later after we finish our meeting with Dahiyas.

At 4pm Dahiya family came. They were not aware of Aditya's predicament. Dhirendra Dahiya asked Aditya what was his aim in life? Aditya answered that he would like to become a General in Indian Army. Out of blind power and enthusiasm, he boasted not to worry, after marrying his daughter, even the Generals would salute him as he might make Aditya the defence minister. Dahiyas were politically very big people so there was more of an ego or false pride problem. Dhirendra Dahiya also offered big money, large area of land and a Jeep as dowry to Karan Veer. The more than anything, by marrying in Dahiya family, the status of the family, would also steep rise.

Karan Veer was not in position to respond but Aditya very politely without disrespecting the Dahiya family told them that he would like to inform that he was already engaged and would request them to arrange a better groom for their daughter. The Dahiya were not ready for this rude shock but since there was not option, they gracefully accepted Aditya request and they became better friends from then onwards. Aditya was born different and he was special.

CHAPTER – 20

Aditya's life in Army and his relationship

The life of Aditya as Captain Indian Army was not a bed of roses, nor did it assure him of all the luxuries of life but it was unmatched. He was very happy for the experience, Indian defence forces offered as they were extraordinary. The honour and the respect of the job along with the privileges gave him the feeling of pride which no other jobs, could offer even on much higher salary package. Life there was hard but he learnt to live life carefree in spite of the uncertainties of tomorrow. While his colleagues were working in air-conditioned offices, Aditya was patrolling for long hours in the scorching Sun, incessant rains or freezing cold with his fellow officers and soldiers. He developed such a strong bond with his colleagues and soldiers that each one of them was prepared to die for each other. He was not married by then but when he heard something like wife swapping in armed forces he got worried. He went in the depth and found out that Army valued and respected everyone's space and never indulged in such practices. Agreed that they were not God sent soldiers and though there morals were expected to be much higher than the rest but again they were not from a different planet and the fact remains that it was never part of either custom or policy of Indian Army. Aditya was very possessive of Jane so he became a bit free from such fear and he decided to get married now.

Aditya was constantly missing Jane and was struggling to maintain his long distance relationship with Jane. He was happy and thankful to present day technology that he was able to speak, see on Skype and talk dirty with his girlfriend. Jane told him that dating a Soldier is difficult but yes, dating Aditya, my Soldier is a commitment. I would get used to being alone. Aditya explained that our relationship now as girlfriend and boyfriend and as husband and wife in future was based on love, trust and respect to each other. It was only for a small period where you might be alone but soon, I would provide you company by giving you the kids, one son and one daughter. Till then just read a book, "The long distance relationship survival guide" by Chris Bell that would keep you with me all the time. Jane replied, "Aditya, I never expected, you could be that dirty. I always thought that you are like an innocuous, tranquil, serene. But you seem to no less than a Volcano which always bears a cryptic smile with notoriety." Aditya responded, "you thought that I am a celibate or ascetic or what? I am a man too dear." Ok, Ok now don't pass those amazing innuendos and monologues and concentrate on your duty" said Jane and Aditya said, "Bye Bye."

Some moments later, Aditya called up Jane and told her that he couldn't resist speaking to her to say that "Relationship is the finest bond between man and woman. It matures with time and passion. It is maintained through connectivity, trust and care. Always allow it to blossom." And to blossom it, "What am I supposed to do, Aditya? "It is very simple. We need 4 hugs a day for survival. We need 8 hugs day for growth." "Leave your job, I will give you 24 hugs a day for a super growth", said Jane. "Stolen kisses are always sweet so bye for now to resume tomorrow night" said Aditya.

CHAPTER – 21

Anwar prepares for IAS

Anwar was working very hard at Rao's Academy in Delhi and Anandita got busy with her Software Development Programme at INFOSYS, Gurgaon. While Anwar was being tutored by the academy, Anandita was also preparing for same at her own. Whenever Anwar asked her to join Rao's Academy, she always used to tell him that she was just taking a chance. Anwar like Aditya always used to tell Anandita, "In life you will realize that there is purpose for every person you meet. Some are there to test you, some will use you and some will teach you and some will bring out the best in you. You are the one, who is doing the last thing to me."

Sometimes, there was a gap, they couldn't meet as either of them was preoccupied. In such situations, Anwar used to get irritated. Anandita used to explain to him that Anwar, your job is tough and you needed perseverance now. "I would keep on meeting you but please let it not become your habit till you qualify your exams." He got more strength and vigour to study harder.

The IAS conducted by UPSC is generally the toughest exam in the world. For selecting 1000 officers the number of applicants is approx.. 9 Lacs. Anwar had almost one year of preparation so he prepared his mind in a disciplined and focused way with a passion for learning and reading. He worked very hard on analytic and presentation skills along with the in depth knowledge of the subjects. He very systematically prepared for both the exam papers. He first concentrated on current events of national and international importance. Collected datas from the toppers, Google. His second challenge was History of India including Indian National Movement. He went into depth of Indian and World Geography including the latest changes, amendments, boundary rows etc. He studied Indian Constitution, latest amendments and governance, Poverty economical and social developments of India, Environmental changes, Sustainability Montreal Protocol and Social responsibility of all the nations including India, China etc.

Karan Veer & Aditya paid Rs.50,000/- to Anwar to purchase all relevant books and other study material like A Modern Approach to Verbal & Non-Verbal reasoning by Mr.Agrawal, India's struggle for Independence by Mr.Mukherjee & Chandra, Certificate Physical and Human Geography by Mr.Leong, our Parliament by Mr.Kashyap, Indian Economy by Mr.Ramesh Singh, cracking the CSAT paper 2 and many more.

He now prepared for paper 2 which consisted comprehension, interpersonal skills including communication skills, logical reasoning, decision making, General mental/ability, basic numeracy, simple mathematical reasoning. Anwar at his own downloaded essay booklet, General Studies booklets 01, 02, 03, 04, 05, 06, 07 and 08 and other subjects of atleast 10 years and learnt them all by heart. He also gathered datas on personal interviews. He revised every subject of paper 2 known as CSAT. It required less hard work compared to paper GS1 but scored high marks, Policy changes every year so Anwar kept himself updated with whatever changes were brought in. he took and cleared IAS Prelims mock exams which gave him the required confidence. He had already purchased all relevant books so it was a great help to him. Throughout the year, he maintained his cool, attended all classes and exams with a relaxed mind.

When the results were announced, Anwar was declared qualified and was placed on Rank 31. He was thoroughly guiding Anandita also. Sometimes they had joint and combined studies and personal discussions and Anwar helped Anandita to the maximum extent possible. Since she was also working in INFOSYS, so she didn't devote that much time as Anwar could do but she also cleared UPSC exam and was placed on 431st Rank. Anwar was sure of being selected for IAS but Anandita had to be contended with IPS.

They both were happy over their achievements and they both wanted to celebrate. Anandita called Anwar at her place for dinner with her parents. The basic idea of inviting Anwar to her place was to judge the reaction of her parents without informing them that they were already in love with each other. As scheduled, Anwar reached their place and he was introduced to her parents as her classmate in IIT Bombay and the fellow who had cleared UPSC IAS category with her. He had secured 31st rank and sure to be selected for IAS training whereas I might be selected for IPS category. Both the parents were highly impressed with the credentials knowingly she also referred Aditya, Karan Veer and his upbringing in Hindu family. She told her father that Papa, Anwar had not only cleared IAS, he had also stood first in UP in a debate competition on GITA when he was in 10th Standard. She was trying her best to paint a picture of Secularism for Anwar but the parents certainly had a bit of reservations for any future thought. They never rejected him outright. Both Anwar and Anandita took it as the first step of victory to their relationship.

They both were asked to report at UPSC house New Delhi for their respective training. Anwar was asked to go to Mussoorie for IAS and Anandita to Hyderabad for IPS training. Anandita submitted her resignation to INFOSYS and was relieved within 15 days. This was another chance for couple to celebrate and this time they both chose "THE AWESOME FARMS and RESORTS, PAKHAL" near Faridabad for a day spending together.

It was expressively understood by both Anwar and Anandita that they were a couple, passionate lovers and future husband and wife. Anwar held her hand and hugged Anandita and she didn't react in anger and this gave Anwar an extra NERVE to touch her. Anwar's hand was gently resting on her cheek while his fingertips slowly moved her neck. The light was switched off and it became completely dark except only few rays of light were coming from door cracks. She was breathing heavily. Anwar was nervous. The man of her dreams leaned over, looked deep into her eyes, gently placed his hands on her chin. They both kissed each other unstoppably. Anwar could sense nothing but the violent beating of his heart. Anandita eyes turned slight pink and red and they didn't face each other for a while out of blush red and blue. It was the most amazing thing ever. He would cherish that moment throughout his life and for Anandita, it was the first date of her Almanac.

CHAPTER – 22

Aditya on Insurgency Mission

Aditya was assigned a specific mission called clean up exercise. He along with his team conducted a major exercise. He along with the elite Meerut based strike corps in desert area near Badmer, Rajasthan wherein the capability to strike deep into enemy territory in an integrated air and land battle environment was evaluated. The focus of the exercise was to achieve joint, seamless and faultless co-ordination among all the forces in a nuclear biological, chemical warfare scenario so as to deliver the enemy, a lethal blow with full might at a lightening speed. The operation was successfully done and Aditya was given his due credit and he became the first force to be on ground in case situation warrants. He was also entrusted the responsibility of training fellow officers and soldiers.

He was given 15 days leave to visit his parents and report at Avantipur, Jammu and Kashmir. As such he was away from Home and Jane specially. Aditya's long distance relationship not only survived but blossomed and it worked spectacularly because it gave both Aditya and Jane the space to grow as individuals while appreciating partners. The lack of proximity and absence of regular communication when normally harm the relationship but in their case, it became more wanting each other and the relationship got more solidified like a igneous rock because they both understood them so well and communicated regularly as and when possible and technology made that easier and they met every alternate months. They always gave it a shot instead of being pessimistic.

Finally the day arrived when they both decided to meet. It was well planned that Aditya after meeting his parents, Shehzadi, Anwar and his bride, would eventually reach Mussoorie where he would be joined by Jane for few days. They would both meet Anwar during his training period over there.

On the appointed day Jane reached Mussoorie and checked in Hotel Hill View which was already booked by Aditya on line.

CHAPTER – 23

Aditya with Jane,
Anwar in Mussoorie

It was a beautiful double bed room on first floor. All they could view from the room was snow clad mountains at long distance and lush green mountains, trees and tiny houses all over. Mussoorie with its green hills and varied Flora and Fauna is a fascinating hills and a famous honeymoon spot. It is famous for its scenic beauty and hectic social life. It is situated in the foothills of the Himalaya ranges known as queen of hills and has a glittering view of Doon valley, Roorkee, Saharanpur & Haridwar. It is situated at an altitude of 2000m, it's a place free from heat of the plains. It is cold in summer and freezing with snow in winter. The rain sights are marvelous and scary at times and stays from July to mid September. It is nicely connected by road and its road from Dehradun to Mussoorie is fantastic and called Serpentine. It is all green when you travel by a cab or bus on that Serpentine road.

Aditya took Jane to almost all the tourist places of attraction namely Kempty falls, Happy Valley, Bhatta Falls and purchased many antiques and wooden handicrafts for Jane.

Jane was very happy and amused throughout their journey to all these places, Aditya did not leave her hand even for a minute. Jane for some moments thought that Aditya was on his honeymoon trip or what?

Aditya very casually asked Jane to tell him with conviction whether she loved him and marry him after three months? Jane replied, "Your question sounds uncalled for and we have discussed this up teen times. I repeat, I will marry you and only you, now, tomorrow or after three months." Now only, said Aditya to which she said, "Aditya, I could feel that you are hinting me something else which I may not agree in Toto." "No, but we are getting married, Aren't we"? asked Aditya. "Yes, we are but we are not married now, Are we?" asked Jane. "Aditya, there are certain moral inhibitions, which are imposing an emergency on my mental status and I certainly would not accede to all your demands".

Aditya pulled her close to his chest and hugged her. He said that he respected Jane for everything. He kissed Jane first very gently on cheeks but later it became a passionate kiss on lips. She felt the heat of his hot lips and warm breaths and couldn't resist responding to his actions. After sometime, she sat against him, her hair tickling his face, gave him an extra nerve. Jane finally melted like butter on hot toasts and finally she couldn't control her moral inhibitions and probably the bodily needs of a woman. "Thank you for everything".

The next day started with a sumptuous breakfast and a kiss of Jane. For Aditya, it was difficult and astounding to put his lips together with Jane though it sounded simple.

Aditya started his research and development and started his explanation to Jane.

"Kissing is a scientific test to test our compatibility. For Jane, it was a critical part of attraction and it increases sexual arousal and it was incredibly important to relationship maintenance. Aditya further explained that scientifically, kissing boosts the production of Oxytocin, the harmone that promotes emotional bonding and inspires feeling of love and affection".

Are you a research scholar or scientist on kissing or what? asked Jane.

"Yes, I am learning and experimenting with you and I feel that kissing you has become a passion and now a crescendo and it is the beginning of intense kissing, replied Aditya".

What was it yesterday then? asked Jane. It was pre-honeymoon rehearsal before we come again for actual one. Ok?

It was high time we have to meet Anwar. Anwar was impatiently waiting to meet both of them. Anwar would be meeting Jane for the first time as Aditya's girlfriend.

Anwar suggested to meet them in officer's mess but Aditya declined and said, we would meet at Neel Kamal Resort as meeting Anwar in his official mess, would be too formal. They all assembled at 4pm at the designated place. Aditya introduced Jane as his girlfriend and future wife and Anwar as his younger brother. Anwar immediately touched Jane's feet as mark of respect for relationship to both Aditya and Jane. Jane enquired about his training progress and also about Anandita. He replied, "Training is going well though tough, and you also know about Anandita? Of course, Aditya had told me all about you and her. He has also told me that she is very beautiful and full of virtues. She is as much intelligent as you Anwar and pursuing her training as IPS trainee". Anwar was amused and said, "Bhabhi, you know much more than me about Anandita but there is still something which you are not aware of and that is, you are more beautiful than her. Aditya says, the opposite. It's true that a man likes his children and other's wives.

Jane found Anwar very matured and like a gangbuster with Aditya's family and she thought that Anwar would make a world of difference for her relationship with Aditya's family.

The city of Mussoorie had entered the month of November when early mornings and evenings carried a huge tinge of winter chill forcing the inhabitants to pack themselves in warm clothes.

After meeting Anwar, they returned to their hotel room. Jane asked Aditya, "what's Anwar's impression about me"? I would repeat exactly what he said about you. Aditya told Jane.

"Jane like any Indian woman, is the most beautiful woman in the world because she is exotic and gorgeous. She is indeed a natural gift to us. She is natural tan giving her a beautiful skin colour. She has raven black hair with beautiful olive black eyes with spark and glow in her eyes. She is shy which makes her attractive. She is friendly, polite and accommodative. She is generally very sweet that enhances her natural beauty. Jane has a caring attitude and can accommodate the entire family. She has the knowledge of our culture by nature. She prefers Sarees in spite of being a Christian. The Saree makes her more exotic and she would also look elegant in Salwar Kameez, dupatta neatly spread and western outfits also."

What was your reaction Aditya when Anwar described my so called beauty? Nothing I simply told him that beauty lies in the eyes of beholder and it is your reflection of enriched human culture, nature and perception of what beauty is. She is beautiful, no doubt from inside and outside as well. I only added that her looks are text book perfect for understanding the features valued on any Indian woman for 1000 years. The best part about Jane is that she has a beautiful soul with a beautiful smile." Anwar also said, which I forgot to tell you, that you are going to help Mom in kitchen, Pooja and maintaining faith in God.

They both returned to their respective places next day morning.

CHAPTER – 24

Aditya marries Jane

After an untiring gaps of two years in insurgency in Kashmir, Arunachal and flood ravaged Uttaranchal, Aditya decided to marry his long time flame Jane and he applied for two months leave. His boss Col. Mukherjee was a kind hearted and a very lenient boss so his leave was sanctioned with a best wishes and congratulatory note. Aditya's marriage with Jane was elaborate and beautiful like a typical North Indian marriage as it was a celebration of all wonderful things in life. Families, Friends, Food, Culture, religion, emotions and most importantly joy all over. Karan Veer arranged lavish decoration and food. He followed all rituals starting from Sagai or the engagement ceremony. Aditya and Jane exchanged rings. Sister Nancy represented the bride side along with Jane's friends. Aditya's father arranged traditional gifts, sweets and dry fruits and tikka material and handed over to Sister Nancy who performed Tikka or engagement ceremony.

On the day before the wedding, Mehndi Ceremony was arranged at both the places. Some nice designs of Mehndi were drawn on Jane's hand and feet and symbolic Mehndi was applied on Aditya's hands also. Music was an important part of such wedding ceremony so a lot of dancing and singing was arranged on Bollywood song themes at both the places.

Actual wedding started in the evening. The groom arrived with lot of fun fair seated on a female horse along with the Baraat, dancing in the midst of crackers and music. The dance form varied from normal Bollywood to any wild form. The bride and groom exchanged garlands with each other called Jaimala ceremony. Lot of fun was created by both the sides to lift the groom high so that the bride could not reach him for garlanding. Same was repeated in case of bride so groom could not garland her but it was all fun and finally garlands were actually exchanged.

Kanyadaan was done by Sister Nancy and Shehzadi to help them. Sat-Phere was the next important ritual and each round or Phera had a different form commitment from both man and woman. Finally the send off was done by Sister Nancy who cried like any mother. Jane came to Mathura along with the Baraat. Next day evening was the reception and before that it was magnanimity of Aditya and his parents to conduct remarriage of both in a typical Christian way. A reception with a large spread of food items ranging from Indian, Chinese and Continental was arranged in Hotel Brajwasi International. A large number of who's who of Mathura and Lucknow were present to grace the occasion and bless the couple. They both became Husband and Wife with their independent identity.

Aditya planned their honeymoon in Kerala. He was not scared of going on war, be it with Pakistan or China but he was scared of going on Honeymoon. He was nervous and so was Jane.

Anyway, Aditya as a man initiated and started exploration of experimental Sex and succeeded for the second time and started explaining to Jane as an expert. "Sexual activities have created a soul tie between me and you Jane. It is not like that super glue called Oxytocin is released in the brains by arriving at Sexual climaxes but even by significant acts of intimacy like holding hands, kissing which also has created the same kind of bonding. The second most important inhibition was the result of so many years of waiting. Aditya waited and waited to convert that NO to YES which Jane couldn't do anymore and she surrendered herself completely thinking that the Bible endorses a concept of Sexual pleasure and assumes a healthy passion. Both Aditya and Jane matured enough to understand Sexuality and Sensuality so they pleasured each other by preparing them for the act. Jane only commented that it was so lovely and beautiful and Aditya, my husband was the best thing that had happened to her. He waited for me and respected and adopted my views on having no premarital Sex.

They visited spice and tea gardens. They also witnessed the Kerala martial art, stayed in house boat and experienced Kerala's special massage and returned to Mathura after a trip of 10 days.

CHAPTER – 25

Anandita in IPS training

The training of Anandita as an IPS trainee was carried out initially for three months at BSNAA in Mussoorie as a basic and foundation course and for one year she attended Phase-I training at NPA Hyderabad. The training involved at Hyderabad was ranging from Normal Policing to counter insurgency Policing in the dense jungles. She was trained in study of Criminal Procedure Code CRPC, Indian Penal Code IPC, Indian Evidence Act and numerous other Indian and foreign laws. She was trained in theoretical and practical ways of conducting investigations. The other subjects which were covered in the training were;

1) Study of Forensic Medicines
2) Internal Security
3) Ethics and Human Rights
4) Maintenance of Public peace and order
5) Information and Communication technology
6) Physical fitness including Sports, PT and cross counting races upto 20Kms
7) Weapon training including assembling etc. for Revolver, SLR, 303 Rifle etc. and hand grenades
8) Map reading of areas

9) Rock climbing
10) Swimming

After a successful training, she was sent to Rajasthan Cadre to join at Jaipur. In between the training, she met Anwar only once but maintaining long distance relationship via Whatsapp, Skype and Mails.

CHAPTER – 26

Anwar & Anandita for Marriage

Anwar after successful completion of his training at both Mussoorie and Hyderabad, was posted as officer on special duty in Home Ministry and he was provided official accommodation at Govt. of India, Greater Kailash, New Delhi. Since he was professionally settled now, Aditya, Jane, Karan Veer, Santosh and Shehzadi wanted him to get married and settle in life. Only Aditya and Jane knew his relationship with Anandita and Anwar was shit scared of informing Karan Veer, Santosh and Shehzadi. He solely depended on Aditya and Jane to see that they all agreed. It would have been very easy for them to convince the elderly clan, if it would not have been intercaste/inter-religion marriage.

Aditya & Jane knew that "marriage between two individuals is due to attraction of bodies which normally is mistaken for love. Love can only be between souls. You are under the impression that Hinduism is more liberal than Islam. Yes, a Hindu might be far liberal than a practicing Muslim and a Muslim might be far liberal than the practicing Hindu."

They also knew that a Muslim can marry a Hindu and she has to;

1) Convert to Islam before marriage
2) Hindu be given a Muslim name
3) Children born to them will have Muslim names
4) Children will undergo SUNAT (Religious circumcision)
5) She will not be allowed to worship idols
6) She will not also be allowed to put Bindi and apply Vermilion (Sindoor)

and much more than even Aditya and Jane knew of. They also had to make efforts to bring both the families on a common platform. They were least informed about Anandita's parents and their reaction. Jane suggested that "before the parents meet, we should arrange one to one meeting between Anwar and Anandita and we should provide them the opportunity to discuss all these issues at their own." Yes, I agree, was Aditya's reply. Aditya called up Anwar and Anandita to meet in Jaipur and discuss their plan keeping in mind the complex issues.

Both Anwar and Anandita met at pool side of hotel Clarks Amer. Nobody from either side accompanied them. Anandita started, "Anwar! I come from a North Indian Rajput family and I am agnostic. I know that you are not a devout Muslim. I also know that you have always respected my religious views and have never coerced or coaxed me into following Islam but my parents are against this relationship."

Anandita - Anwar, I am frightened and need your assurance that your parents would never force me to convert and eat beef.

Anwar - I have only a poor Muslim mother and Hindu parents (Aditya's father & mother). My mother will never force you to convert and eat beef.

Anandita - Anwar, for the sake of love, can you willingly leave Islam and convert to Hinduism?

Anwar - First of all we would remain as two human beings married to each other. But in case of non-acceptance of us by this society, we would both get converted into Buddists.

Anandita - We would not covert to either Islam or Hinduism but we would maintain our individual identities. We might consider conversion of our children to Buddhism. But Islam doesn't allow Muslims to marry Non-Muslims. Then what.

Both of them agreed to discuss the entire case in front of Anandita's parents, Aditya's parents and Anwar's mother. They both were very senior Govt. Servants, matured enough but were not in position to take the call.

A meeting was arranged in Mathura after a week wherein the people from both sides would be present.

Anandita went to meet her parents and discussed before the meeting with third party. After giving it a very deep thought, Anandita's father said that, "BETA, if you want to do love marriage, we don't have any concerns. But please make sure that your future husband and his family, has similar thinking and culture as our family. In a Muslim family, you have to follow their culture. There would also be ceremonies at BAKRID and other festivals which may not be OK with you. Next big problem, you will face and would not be able to digest the rituals which they would have on your new born baby. If that new born is a girl child, God save you from the pains, your child will undergo, when she would be 5 or 6 years, called FGM (Female Genital Mutilation).

Marrying Anwar is not only the relationship between you and Anwar, it is the relationship of two families rather three families. We have our reservations that this marriage will involve the healthy and interacting families. Beta, we are staying in Western Civilization. Religions are made for a reason and marrying in other religions can jeopardize an existence of religion in you. Understanding and hearing her parents, Anandita was getting cold feet.

Karan Veer, Santosh, Shehzadi, Akbar and his wife Gul joined Aditya and Jane at Dampier Hotel lounge. An hour later Anandita came with her parents. They were introduced by Aditya and Anandita. Anandita's parents felt a little consoled after seeing the Hindu guardians of Anwar. Surendra Singh, Anandita's father expressed his concerns regarding the conversion and various Islamic rituals which

Anandita would find difficult to follow and even we as family. Every point right from conversion, beef, change of name and kids their Sunat or FGM, was pointed out by the parents and they wanted the clarification and commitment from Anwar's family and Karan Veer's family.

Even when both the people, Anwar and Anandita were matured and established in the Society on very senior positions of authority but Surendra Singh wanted the reply from the seniors of the families. Shehzadi was not educated and all her decisions of life, were taken by Santosh and Karan Veer, she left these answers also to be given by them only. Though Karan Veer was responsible for Anwar's upbringing and bringing him to this position, he was finding it difficult to satisfy all Surendra Singh's apprehensions. Religion being a sensitive issue, he could not take decision on the issue.

He simply said, "Anwar, you are an IAS officer and Anandita an IPS officer; you both would find numerous such cases of conflict and you both would be using your good sense and would find an amicable and just solution without any prejudice to law and Constitution of India." Why don't both of you only suggest the right way and a step forward. "You both decide whether love takes over religion or religion becomes priority and checks love?" Anwar and Shehzadi univocally said, "we cannot decide but would respect your advice. After all Anwar is like Aditya for you." Anandita also seconded Anwar. Karan Veer discussed with Aditya and joined the discussion.

He addressed Surendra Singh and Aarti Singh, "Anwar has grown in our home along with Aditya and my four daughters. Since I am father of four daughters, so all interest of your daughter are important to us. He has been brought up as a human, then a Muslim or Hindu. He respects all religious. He celebrates all our Hindu Festivals as a family and we have never noticed even an iota of difference in his feelings for both Hindu and Muslim. He can recite Gita and Ramayan better than Aditya and Aditya in his company is also aware of Quran and its verses. My son goes to Mosque with Anwar and he goes to temples with Aditya and nobody so far has differentiated between Aditya and Anwar.

I would stand guarantee that Anandita would not be forced to convert and follow Islamic rituals which she would not like to do like we have never enforced our views on Anwar and his family. They both can retain their independent identities and decide their way of life.

We are aware of that many jilted people would want to give it a tag of love Jihad but knowing both Anwar and Anandita who are much above the hurdle of religious bias and they both are humans first then Muslim and Hindu. We both, Aditya and me would stand like a China Wall against such unscrupulous, self-styled parasites of the society and we both would also check the caste divide and eruption of the socio political volcano. His assurance, gave both Surendra and Aarti a big feeling of relief and everyone left the decision on Anwar and Anandita.

The issues were coming to a logical end but Gul's sudden outburst created a big flutter. She unexpectedly said to Anandita, "Anandita, we are not aliens or have come from some other planets. Also you are not going to make history in India or the Islamic World or the rest of World by being the first Hindu female converting to Islam. There are up teen number of cases in the past and will be in future. So, I don't think that you should not covert to Islam to marry Anwar. Shehzadi got wild and asked Gul to shut up and said when two elders of the family are talking, your views are not that important. Let Thakur Saab (Karan Veer) take the decision.

Gul's utterance for sure, gave jolt to all including Anandita and her parents. Anyway decision now was left on both Anwar and Anandita.

CHAPTER – 27

Aditya visits Rudaalis

Aditya was to join duty after a week so he took Jane with him to Jaisalmer. He contacted Aftab, his college friend. He informed him that he would like to visit the desert fair and also like to resume his unfinished work of bringing some changes in the lives of those Rudaali women. He specifically mentioned the name of an young Rudaali widow girl for whom he had arranged her entire education with the help of an NGO through Sister Nancy and he himself was a devoted soldier for its uplift.

Aditya and Jane took morning flight from Delhi to Jodhpur and then hired an air-conditioned cab from Jodhpur to Jaisalmer which is approx.. 300 Kms from Jodhpur. Jaisalmer is well connected to the rest of state by well maintained roads. Since it is close to Indo-Pak border so Aditya ensured that the cab he hired was brand new and also ensured that they reach before Sunset. They booked themselves in Desert National Park.

They drove down from Jodhpur and reached the Hotel at 6pm.

Unlike Delhi and Mumbai, Jaisalmer has little nightlife but has a lot of fun in form of traditional dances, a desert light show and some in-house evening entertainment for the guests. This hotel also had its private discotheques which was open till early mornings. It also had a rich pub or bar which could serve the finest French wines both red and white.

Aftab also joined them next day morning and they planned their local tour including the Camel Safari. Jane initially didn't like and felt too bumpy but subsequently she was not prepared to leave that. They also visited Desert Cultural Centre, Gadsisar lake, Jain temple, Jaisalmer Fort and Nathmalji ki Haveli and clicked lot of pics of all of them. They felt hungry and had lunch at TRIO. It is one of the most famous Restaurant serving authentic Rajasthani Cuisines. Jane for the first time witnessed the traditional reception. The welcome team applied Tilak and garlanded them. The food was nice and of typical signature of the desert.

Then they had gone to Jaisalmer Desert Festival which is an annual event organized by the Rajasthan Tourism Development Corporation. Dressed in vibrant and colourful attire, the people of Rajasthan sing and dance to lingering ballads of heroism, romance and tragedy of yore. Fire works explode across the sky, splashing with colours bring the fort to life.

Jane also enjoyed many events such as camel racing, turban tying and the longest mustache competition and also different cultural wonders of Rajasthan. They were too tired so just retired.

Next day Aftab arranged a meeting between Salma, her aunt with Aditya. Salma was the same young Rudaali girl who became a widow as a child and Aditya had arranged her education through one NGO. Now even Jane wanted to support her in all her future achievements. She felt very happy to see Aditya's this gesture. She just hugged Aditya and started waiting for Salma.

Finally Salma came dressed in all white Salwar Kameez with blue dupatta. She was approx.. 14 years, very good looking, fair and smart girl. Aditya introduced him and his wife Jane. Salma said, "I know you from last seven years. You came to my house and met my mother-in-law. I also remember so clearly that you were the one who advised and arranged my admission in St. Anne's Convent School, Jaisalmer. Thank you so much on behalf of my entire family of Rudaalis otherwise even I would have grown up mourning for others professionally. My entire clan is indebted to you as you have shown up the light to move from our dark corridor. Now there are twelve girls studying from class 1st to 4th.

Aditya   - Which standard are you in now?

Salma   - I am in IXth Standard.

Jane   - What do you become in life now and why?

Salma   - I would like to become an advocate so that I
           could fight and support people like me to see the
           modern day world.

Aditya   - What do you expect me and Jane Aunty to do
           for you?

Salma   - Please keep on visiting me and all the Kids like
           me, just to inspire. Your NGO is supporting all
           of us financially and emotionally.

Jane   - Salma, I have also experienced similar
           environment and ambience in my life like yours.
           Just work your best. Aditya and me, would
           always be with you. Aditya would work for you
           to come up in life and he would like to see you
           as an established attorney.

Salma   - Thank you both so much and I have now a deep
           bond with you.

Aditya   - I still have a lot to do for Rudaalis and would
           like to see all of them flourishing not vanishing.

Both Aditya and Jane came back to Mathura and Aditya left
to Assam to take charge of his professional duties. Aditya
indeed was born different. He was special.

CHAPTER – 28

Anwar & Anandita discuss marriage

All the options were explored by both Anwar and Anandita once again based on the discussion, views, out of that family get-together last week but certainly they did not reach to an amicable solution. They both consulted advocates to understand the laws related with inter faith marriages. They both agreed that the most ideal way would be for both Anwar and Anandita, to get their marriage registered under the Special Marriage Act. Under this acts, no conversion would be required by either of them but the biggest problem would be that Islam forbids Muslims from marrying Non-Muslims. Though such registered marriage would be perfectly valid according to the laws of India but such a marriage would not be a marriage under Muslim religious code and would be considered as an adulterous relationship.

Anandita also got scared for his kids and some rituals. Also the anticipated problems of Society like names of children, attitude of Non-Muslims towards Muslims in the present environment, she asked Anwar whether it would work peacefully, Anwar? This is not an arrangement for months or years. This is going to be for our life time so let us take this decision today after giving it a serious thought. I know that we both love each other and I do not doubt your perseverance for our welfare but again this world is so cruel and intolerant. I also know that you will not PROSELYTISE, me to change.

Anwar very innocently and simply said, "If it is your birth right to follow your religion so would be mine, may be not with that intensity as preached in Islam. I do not have any intentions to convert you or get converted. It is not necessary that we get married. I loved you and would still love you."

"I knew it as I know you Anwar more than you know yourself," said Anandita. We both are responsible citizens and have lot of things to do in life. Presently we take a decision that we would not marry each other. Let time and destiny decide about our lives as husband and wife. Anwar said, "I would not marry now and join our PM's brigade."

Anandita said, "I will leave this in God's and my parents' hands. I know, Aditya and his parents, will be disappointed but at least my parents will sigh a feeling of relief. They were worried, Anwar, as I am the only child of them."

They both promised to remain friends for ever after this. They both conveyed their discussions to their respective families. Aditya, though felt bad, but was sure that the decision taken by both of them would be in their interest.

CHAPTER – 29

Jane shares News

Aditya was posted at Nalhu La in Eastern Sikkim near the shrine of Baba Harbhajan Singh who died in line of his duties as an Adjutant. It is believed that his spirit protects every soldier in that inhospitable high attitude terrain of Eastern Himalayas. Aditya's task force was guarding the 3488 Km SINO-INDIAN border and his posts were in some of the hardest areas with locations ranging from 9000 ft to 18000 ft where the temperature goes below 0 degree Celsius. Aditya's camp was provided with some ultramodern SUVs along INDO-CHINA border for the first time. Before Aditya was posted on this border, he was sent to attend a seminar called BORDER MANAGEMENT GUARDING THE FRONTIERS which was concluded by CENTRE FOR LAND WELFARE STUDIES (CLAWS). The training was imparted by the cream of THINKTANKS and experts from Indian Army and Bureaucracy. He was given responsibility to manage all unresolved and disputed borders. Aditya was on 24 hour duty on highest battle ground at INDO-CHINA border at minus 50 degree Celsius temperature. He made his battalion a good team and his family. His life was a lot tough which can't be explained but can be experienced. They were always scared of the enemy bullets from any direction and weather conditions and sometimes the life of Aditya was really frustrating. He only had a small room called Bunker to relax and talk to his family if luck favoured.

Jane wanted to share a news with her husband. Announcing your big news can be one of the most meaningful and just fun part of the pregnancy. She knew under what stringent conditions, Aditya was working but even this was important.

Under these conditions, Aditya got a call from Jane. Holding his heart tightly, he answered.

Aditya   - Hi Jane, How are you?

Jane   - I am good. I have some news for you.

Aditya   - Have you been promoted or what?

Jane   - No. It is bigger than that.

Aditya   - I can't wait. Tell me Jane.

Jane   - I am expecting. Isn't that wonderful?

Aditya   - It is much more than just wonderful. When, Where, How? Give me the total report.

Jane   - I am collecting the report tomorrow then I'll let you know.

Aditya   - Take good care of you and my baby.

Jane   - I will.

Aditya woke up all his buddies and shared this news and the celebration started at the dead night. His battalion fired 10 rounds of ammunition as a mark of happiness.

CHAPTER – 30

Anwar, Anandita on their jobs

Anwar resumed his duties at Ministry of Home Affairs, Delhi with the task of controlling terrorism and the spread of their bases in India. The neighbouring country was having a very hostile attitude and was trying their best to plan maximum damage to people and property. Anwar during a course of investigation, also noticed that there is a conduit for supply of narcotics drugs from Pakistan to India, India to Bangladesh and African countries. He with the help of Mumbai/Delhi Police smashed the racket.

Anwar made certain policy changes and with the help of Govt. of INDIA, Politicians and Police in such a way that the infiltration of terrorists and drug peddlers was minimized. In the process of performing his duties, he was offered a lot of bribe in terms of money and also reminding him that he was a Muslim and it was his duty to help Muslim brothers to create problems and disturb peace of the State. He was a true nationalist and such petty things didn't attract his conscience to act against such greed.

Ananadita over there in Jaipur was entrusted the duties of improving the conditions of Jails all over Rajasthan without compromising any security risk. She prepared a Jail Manual which was not only implemented in Rajasthan and other Indian Jails but was recognized in international policing. She was honoured by President's medal for her meritorious service. The normal and hardcore criminals also appreciated the efforts.

Based on her performance as Dy. S.P. Jails and also a Policy maker for Jail reforms, she was promoted as Deputy Commissioner Police (DCP), Internal Security and also to deal with the challenges of terrorism, Insurgency, Communalism and Caste Violence. Her basic responsibilities involved her direct co-ordination with National Investigation Agency (NIA) and Interpol. Within a short span of time, she became quite popular and people started comparing her with Kiran Bedi.

Away from their official chores and in spite of their resolution that they would not marry, there was the highest form of bondage between Anwar and Anandita. Anwar remembered that he took extreme delight in spending time with Anandita, his love for her was beyond compare but the moment, he heard Anandita saying No to their marriage, sent shock waves in his spine and a heavy cloud of grief hanged over both of them. They both spent sleepless nights for up teen numbers of days. Before that decision, they both met there for few moments without a word.

Anandita for the call of her duties towards her parents refused marriage to Anwar but she thought to herself that nothing could take Anwar way from her even when he left her physically. She was all the time living the life of contemplation thinking about Anwar. She had no place for anything else in her life except work. However there was constant pressure of marriage by her mother.

Years rolled by she wanted to meet Anwar one more time in her life. Even Anwar wanted to meet her once in his life so destiny provided them an opportunity for a meeting on internal security at New Delhi, chaired by the Home Minister. Even after a lot of time had passed in between them they needed no words to replenish their relationship. They could both know that none of them got married in life so far.

They both realized that "most love affairs in India are victim of barriers created by Caste/Religion/Family or Society and Love is not done intentionally, it just HAPPENS. You cannot stop love and feelings for someone, no matter how hard you try. But there is no option.

Anandita was awarded the Ramon Magsaysay award recognizing her leadership and innovations in crime control drug rehabilitation and humane prison reform.

CHAPTER – 31

Jane delivers Twins

Aditya purchased a house in Civil lines, Mathura which is located halfway up to a quiet hill called Govardhan and surrounded by nature. It is just 15 minutes short stroll from Krishna-Janmabhoomi and Mathura Railway Station. There are numerous excellent restaurants, supermarkets and theatres.

The house was nicely decorated to the taste of an army officer and exotic ultramodern interiors designed by Jane. All rooms had Air-conditioners and fans fitted and also attached bathrooms. Kitchen had all modular furniture and ranges.

This was meant for Jane to stay after coming from Roorkee and joining a premier engineering college in Mathura as Lecturer. Her in-laws used to be week end visitors.

Jane's doctor after conducting various tests and ultrasonic tests confirmed that Jane carried twins and the doctor didn't reveal the sex of the babies in spite too much of pleading by both husband and wife. She used to go for normal check-ups regularly.

The D,day was fast approaching. Aditya was granted special leave after a long tough job to be with his wife.

Aditya was more tensed than the lady who would be delivering the babies. They were advised to give birth in a hospital as there could be a higher chance of complications with twins. The hospital was asked to arrange a midwife, an obstetrician and two pediatricians one for each baby. The doctor explained to both Aditya and Jane that a lot of women think that they would be required to have a caesarean section with twins but more than 40 percent of all twins are born vaginally, normal delivery and the process is similar to that of a single baby. As Aditya was born as a breach baby, he was more worried so the Doctor recommended to have an EPIDURAL for pain relief. Final decision would be taken at the time of birth and Aditya specifically was advised to keep away from Jane. Only Santosh, Jane's mother-in-law would remain present. Finally it was observed that space occupied by twins was more so only one baby was postured as head down.

The delivery was conducted as Caesarean one and the twins were born and Jane gave births to twin male, healthy children. The happiest person on earth was the grandmother. She distributed sweets to the entire staff and other patients. She also gave Rupees one thousand to all involved in the delivery. Jane took both the babies in her lap and said, "Oh, they are so identical and I am now seeing two mini Adityas. Aditya felt proud and happy.

The author wants to know from readers whether for this also he has to say, Aditya is born different. He is special?

Jane stayed in the hospital for 10 days. Aditya arranged Twin baby accessories and clothes. After 10 days, there were celebrations all over including his own village. Sister Nancy came to see and to bless the babies.

CHAPTER – 32

Naming ceremony & celebrations

India is very rich in the customs and traditions which keeps its people binding together. The arrival of the twins in the family was a big joyous celebrations specially for Karan Veer and Santosh. They organized this function on such a large scale to establish their name and fame, that it was considered to be biggest of last twenty years. The purpose was NAMKARAN (Naming Ceremony). According to Hindu mythology, the naming ceremony for the new born takes place on the twelfth day after the birth and generally considered to be a ladies function but Aditya's parents made it big by inviting ladies and gentlemen of neighbouring seven villages to witness the naming ceremony and have DAAVAT (Lunch). On the appointed day female relatives and friends also arrived to participate in the colourful ceremony. Anwar came specially from Delhi to bless the newly born along with his mother and sister-in-law.

Both the twins were placed in two Jhulas (Cradles), decorated with colourful flowers and ribbons. All the women gathered around Jhulas and sang traditional naming ceremony songs. Traditionally again, Aditya's sisters held the four corners of the cloth on which both the babies were lying in the cradles. Then they gently did swinging the cloth to give movement to the cradles while the ladies continued singing and dancing. One of the women jokingly asked Aditya's sisters, how would they know, whether the new born twins were boys or girls? The sisters without any hesitation uncovered the cover of the babies and said "Satisfy yourself and the differentiate in male and female yourself. The entire gathering split in loud laughter.

The Panditji (Brahmin who performs Pooja) started the holy fire (HAVAN) and the chanting of holy Sanskrit Shlokas started. It continued for one hour along with the traditional singing and swinging of Jhulas. Aditya and Jane were sitting in Pooja with Panditji. Aditya in his light yellow DHOTI and Jane in light yellow Saari, with wet hair and Sindoor were looking gorgeous and Jane more devotional rather than epitome of beauty. She was naturally beautiful and her beauty got amplified after the birth of her twin sons. All singing and dancing were being conducted and co-ordinated by Aditya's youngest sister.

Hindus often prefer to names their children based on Hindu Rashis because it is considered auspicious and supposed to bring good fortune to the children. After the Pooja and dance sequence, the twins were named as DEV and VED on mutual consent from Panditji, grandparents, parents and Aditya's sisters.

A huge Pandal was erected and a nice, sumptuous lunch with lot of items were served to 1700 people. Actually it was grandparents day. Aditya and Jane liked the names very much. DEV and VED have same alphabets and are religious names.

CHAPTER – 33

Time takes leap of 3 years and then 5 years

Now since the boys DEV and VED were already three, Jane had something that was very near and dear to her heart, was getting her children "SCHOOL READY". She thought that now her sons would be attending pre-school in next one week and that would be their first school experience and also Jane's first experience as a Twin Mama.

The biggest challenge and anxiety filled situation was getting her twin ready for their first day at school. She started thinking and imagining whether they would be Ok? Would they make friends in School? Would they learn in School? All these questions were racing in her mind and she thought that all the children came home happy with a smile on their faces wherein my case they are twins unlike other children. My twins will be best friends in themselves. Even if they are placed in different classrooms, they still would have that sense of security.

With these thoughts in her mind, she was leaving them every day to Pre-school and was picking them after the school for few weeks. Initially they cried but once they saw too many kids, they started enjoying it. Even the teachers in the Pre-school enjoyed their togetherness. Soon they grew up to join Standard Ist after clearing Playgroup, Lower K.G., Upper K.G.

As Aditya and Jane both wanted these boys to become strong and independent, they were admitted in Indian Army Public School, Mathura. These Schools are generally managed by the Army Regional Commanders following the CBSE Pattern of Education. Admissions are granted on a priority basis to the wards of army personnel. All Army Public Schools have a Chairman who is a Senior Indian Army Officer of Brigadier Rank and a Patron who is of a Major General Rank.

The Schools are rich in terms of study, infrastructure, atmosphere and a much deeper feel of Nationalism and responsibility.

The boys were being shaped in an intelligent and disciplined ambience. Aditya one day asked DEV and VED who is easy to communicate, Maa or Papa? Adrib, came the reply from both, PAPA of course because MOM is very very strict." Jane smiled and said "He is lenient because he is hardly at home."

Their studies were also being monitored by Jane on daily basis. The advantage Jane had was that the medium of teaching in army public school was English and they were following the common syllabus and course of study.

CHAPTER – 34

Anwar comes home & meets Aditya and Jane

One day Shehzadi complained of severe and excruciating chest pain in early hours of the morning and Akbar was not immediately available as he had gone to some other city to buy some advanced seeds of Wheat and also some spare parts for tractor repairs. Gul rushed to Santosh and briefed her about Shehzadi's condition. Karan Veer and Santosh wasted no time and took her in a tractor and admitted her in District Civil Hospital, Mathura. Jane joined them after sending the kids to School and arranged full medical care including angiography and there were three major blockages in main arteries.

Anwar came on 3 months of sick leave to provide care for a family member with a serious health conditions. Akbar also joined his mother in the hospital. Anwar in consultation with Jane, Karan Veer and Akbar took a decision to get the operation done without any loss of time. The angioplasty was done successfully and Shehzadi came back home after 9 days and then a good care taken by Akbar & Gul specially on food and medication. On hearing Shehzadi's operation, Aditya came on four days leave.

After visiting and reassuring Shehzadi his second mother, Aditya came to his house at Mathura along with Anwar.

In the evening, both Aditya and Anwar were sitting in the lawn and were discussing their official matters. Jane joined them. The discussion raised from work to relationship and then to Anandita.

Jane — Anwar, How is Anandita? Are you guys in touch with each other?

Anwar — No idea Bhabhi, I have not seen her or talked to her for years now. She is a lady with a very strong mind.

Aditya — Did you try to talk to her? After all she must have melted and priorities must have changed.

Anwar — I am keeping a track of her wellbeing, Aditya. After all, indirectly she is reporting to the Ministry of Home Affairs. She is doing very well Aditya, professionally.

Jane — Anwar, do you think, I shall talk to her someday?

Anwar — No Bhabhi, she has not married and keeping everything to herself. Now her work has become her worship.

Aditya - I feel, I should talk to her father, Mr.Surendra Singh and should try to study her mind from him.

Anwar - You could talk to him. On my last official meeting with her, she was also remembering you and she respects you the most.

Jane - Aditya, you please sort it out by talking to her father or to her but all I want, Anwar to settle down in life. I also wish Anandita to settle down. She is a very cute baby for me.

Aditya - Anwar, you are still there for some more days, we will meet after two days. Till then, you take care of your MOM.

Anwar left the place, to be with his mother. He didn't use the official machinery like local police and administration for his personal gain.

Aditya called up Mr.Surendra Singh and discussed the matter of Anandita and Anwar. He very categorily told Aditya that he had allowed Anandita to take all decisions regarding Anwar in whatever way, she thought. We are prepared to accept her choice any way. But she has decided not to talk for any alliance with Anwar or with anybody. She said last time, nothing mattered to her in this world more than her old parents and it was never necessary that everybody on earth had to marry compulsorily. If we ever asked her, what after us, she only told, "I would marry my work or any NGO which would finish this caste and religion system.

Aditya thanked them for the information but told them that he would certainly talk to Anandita once before accepting defeat. Next day, he called up Anandita and invited her to his place. She agreed to meet Aditya, Jane and kids but she requested that they would not discuss their marriage plans to Anwar. She also agreed to meet Anwar but with no intentions of changing her mind.

Since Jaipur is just three hours from Mathura so Anandita drove down to Aditya's place. She met everybody including Anwar but nothing of that sort happened which could have made Aditya, Jane and Anwar happy. She was very happy to meet Jane and two kids. She had dinner with them and left for Jaipur late evening. She also exchanged greetings with Anwar and nothing hard or harsh was noticed from both of them.

CHAPTER – 35

After another gap of one year

The boys were growing and glowing and were in Standard IInd now. They were very popular in school with their friends and teachers. They were both watching their father in uniform so the passion of wearing uniform came to their hearts and minds since early childhood. Aditya and Jane wanted them to become Engineers after graduating from some premier engineering institutes in India and then masters from some foreign universities but they used to tell their parents that they would love to do engineering from India but after completing engineering from India, they would like to join Indian armed forces.

Jane once suggested both of them to study medicines and become doctors to which they both replied in one voice, "Maa, in case we both would have been female twins, yes we would have accepted it but we are MARDS so army officers with engineering background like dad would be fine." Ok my little Mards and hugged her children.

Salma after completing her graduation joined SBK Govt. College, Jaisalmer in law faculty for two years course in law. She had already cleared her 12th and Graduation securing good percentage so her admission for doing LLB, was not a problem.

There was a tremendous transformation in Salma from a Rudaali girl to a well educated, well mannered girl. Aditya noticed that Salma had grown up to be a most beautiful girl, dressed in white top and blue jeans. She was having long, lustrous black hair making plaits. She was bearing simple ear rings, few bangles and chain in the neck. She applied very light make-up and lipstick. When Aditya met Salma, she briefed him regarding her studies, general progress of her career. When Jane asked him to describe Salma after so many years, he described Salma as under.

Salma has typical Rajasthani eyes, large typically almond shaped, dark and expressive framed with long lashes under slender dark eyebrows and heavily lined with Kajal. She was having a sense of responsibility and respectful behavior. Culturally she had manners, dignified body language and good verbal language. She is 5 feet 7 inches tall, fair and clear skin and has athletic built.

Such a girl when her temper is good, her nature kindly, her sleep short and her mind and body not inclined to laziness, should at once be married by a wise man. Who could be a better choice than Anwar? He suggested and Jane agreed. Aditya checked with Salma for he could think on these lines. Her Aunt said, yes, we would discuss with Anwar when he would be staying with us.

Anwar was selected to join U.N. on deputation from Ministry of Home Affairs. He agreed for two years tenure which could also provide him international exposure.

Aditya thought that even Salma needed two years to complete her law degree. Anandita was awarded Ramon Magsaysay Award and nominated as Police Advisor to Secretary General of United Nations but she refused citing some personal reasons owing to her parents at home (Anwar could be another reason).

Adding to these sequence of events, there was one more addition. Aditya after a long service in hard areas, was transferred to 33rd ARMOURED DIVISION Headquartered in Mathura. His this division basically controls Infantry, Mountain Division and 33rd Armoured Division. Now he was close to his family and could concentrate on his domestic issues like parents, agriculture, Akbar & family and Anwar in particular. Jane and kids were very happy on this change.

CHAPTER – 36

Anwar with Aditya before U.N. Duties

Both Aditya and Jane were sitting in a tranquil, serene mood in their lawns with some tea and biscuits. Both DEV and VED were playing right in front of them. It was Sunday afternoon. Jane after a good bath and shampooed hair, was looking very radiant and ravishing. Aditya left no chance to be close to her but a simple excuse of kids being there, kept him at a distance.

In fact, they were waiting for Anwar to come for dinner and drinks as Anwar was to leave for Germany for almost two years on an U.N. assignment. Aditya also wanted to navigate to his mind to know whether he was prepared to marry now under the changed circumstances when Anandita had already very clearly communicated of not marrying Anwar or anybody.

Anwar was very dear to both Aditya and Jane, so they wanted him to somehow get married and settle in life. He also remembered his promise to Santosh, his mother and

Shehzadi, Anwar's mother that he would ensure that Anwar would marry after Anandita Fiasco.

Anwar came at 7pm. Jane prepared some nice food like Chicken Biryani and other luscious and tasty starters with the drinks for these two brothers. Both Aditya and Jane were concealing and camouflaging their cryptic smiles. Anwar as usual was ignorant of their plan of action. They basically wanted to discuss his marriage proposal and were weaving a Chakravuh for him. Poor chap, was going in the web of their plans.

As an IAS officer, Anwar, you look quite dignified. We all feel very proud of your these achievements.

Anwar   - No, Bhai, I am so grateful to you Aditya for everything, you have done for me. I will always remain indebted to you for life time.

Aditya   - Anwar you are too modest.

Anwar   - If I have to pay for debt by even giving my life, I'll do it. I will do it for you, Aditya, for Maa, my Maa too.

Aditya   - I will give you a chance to clear my debt. Don't worry.

Aditya asked Jane to get the picture of Salma and give it to Anwar. Aditya asked Anwar to see the picture. Anwar had a good look on the picture and there was a stoic silence for few moments. Aditya said, "Anwar, today is the day, you are in authority to refuse and I would respect your refusal because it is the question of your life time but if I have to ask you something today, it would be like asking you to marry, Salma who is widowed from her childhood and staying in an Ashram (Charity Home) and pursuing her LLB from Jaisalmer. She is daughter of Rudaali and all her education is being sponsored by an NGO through me. I am not forcing you to accept my request but I will call them next week at my place. You will meet her, discuss with her and let me know. She has two years to complete her law and even you have two year's commitment."

CHAPTER – 37

Aditya arranges a meeting for Anwar & Salma

After Aditya got convinced that photos of both Anwar and Salma were accepted as approved individually by both of them, Aditya invited Salma with her Aunt and Anwar at his place. Two days after the meeting took place. Aditya introduced Anwar to Salma and Salma to Anwar. Aditya also informed Salma about Anandita and Anwar and their past love story. He very clearly informed Salma that they could have married about an year back, had the religion would not have come in between. Anandita was from a ritual Hindu family. He also informed Anwar that Salma was a Rudaali girl and now she is pursuing law course. "Salma is as part of me and Jane as you are." Salma became widow at the age of 5 years. Opportunity was given for the boy and girl to speak privately aside in a balcony sit out. They both discussed their present and past, their occupation, job family members. They both seemed compatible so it was considered to be nice if both of them could marry.

Jane asked Anwar "Whether things would work out?" Anwar replied – I would never disrespect my brother's wish. Even you wanted it Bhabhi, didn't you?

Aditya asked Salma and her aunt. The reply was positive. Salma said, "you have always played a role of a guardian and my elder brother so I would always respect your wish very gladly and Anwar is a dignified gentleman."

Jane said to Aditya – Aditya you are born different and you are special.

CHAPTER – 38

Anwar weds Salma
after two years

Arranged marriage is scary for sure but things really work well. Both Anwar and Salma had invested it as a relationship. Their base of relationship was respect because they both believed that the one who couldn't respect you, couldn't love you unconditionally. They might have many ups and downs in their life and times to come but what would hold their relationship in place would be trust, respect and friendship between two.

Aditya called his friend after two weeks to conduct the marriage of Anwar with Salma as he wasn't fully aware of the systems in Islamic marriage. Aftab was assisted by Akbar, his wife Gul and his mother Shehzadi. According to Aftab, the marriage in Islam is considered and viewed as a religious obligation, a contract between the couple and Allah. The only requirement for Islamic marriage, the marriage contract was signed by both Anwar and Salma. The marriage was conducted at home and no clergy was required as Aftab was aware of the entire Islamic traditions to officiate the wedding. The MEHER, the monetary amount as discussed and agreed, was paid by Anwar to Salma. Actually the MEHER is the Security/ Guarantee amount for the bride. Anwar also presented a diamond ring to her as engagement/MEHER. Both the bride and groom heard the religious ceremony recital called FATIHAH as they were asked to listen and understand the meaning of marriage and their responsibilities to each other and Allah.

NIKAH, the marriage contract was signed by both of them in front of witnesses Akbar and Aditya.

The marriage was concluded and a grand reception was hosted by Aditya in their honour on a reasonably good scale. He invited all the IAS and IPS fraternity, important people of the district and capital. Aditya played a wonderful role and bid a grand send off to her younger sister Salma. She cried inconsolably by keeping her head on Aditya and Jane's shoulders.

Aditya was born different. He was special.

CHAPTER – 39

Aditya after a Party

Last night Aditya had a party with his officers in Army mess for celebrating the tally of medals his infantry division earned from 1965, 1971 and 1999 Indo-Pak wars. The party was grand, nice food, standard Scotland whisky and French red and white wines. He returned late along with Jane. By that time, the kids were fast asleep.

That night he dreamt that Almighty God had put him in a God synchronous orbit on a journey which never ended as its final destination was ETERNITY.

He woke up late, quite disturbed and when Jane asked him about this, he only said that, "He has certain unfinished jobs to do which he has neglected for a very long time. Until unless, he makes a time bound programme, he will not be able to accomplish them."

Next day, Aditya suddenly visited all his old friends and relatives. He even visited those people, whom he normally would have not visited. Few days later he purchased two Life Insurance policies for his sons which was absolutely unplanned. He called up his parents and sisters. He drew his

WILL, authorizing Jane to take all decisions related with all the properties, bank balance, agricultural land of his name. He wanted to meet Anwar, Salma and Anandita. He also expressed desire to meet one of his professors, Mr.Anand Bhide of IIT Roorkee whom he had not met for almost 10 years. Whatever he was doing or was proposing to do, was all unprecedented and unexpected but Jane always thought that Aditya was born different and he was special so up to maximum extent, she digested but the moment he talked about taking Jane for lunch, then to movie and then to Roorkee to meet sister Nancy, Jane became a bit-uncomfortable. She agreed for whatever he wanted. One more unusual thing that happened the same night was that he insisted of getting even his kids in his bedroom to sleep with him and Jane.

There was something unusual now. She was worried for some unanticipated incident though she was quite fearless and valiant in nature. She looked up in the mirror as the tears that had settled around the curvature of her eyes like thin beads ran like an overflown stream over her cheeks. Aditya noticed them and asked, "why are you crying?" She said "it is because of some insects in eye." "Stop running from yourself from what your heart says" said Aditya. Her face was then a unique blend of beauty, sensuousness and maturity.

They both had an uncomfortable sleep that night.

CHAPTER – 40

Indian Army cancelled leave

Indian Army cancelled leave of all army personnel, officers and soldiers with tension rising between India & Pakistan on the line of control (LOC). India decided to cancel all bus services from India to Pakistan and back. All diplomatic channels of communication with Pakistan were shut.

Aditya was asked to report at Jammu at the earliest. Aditya with a heavy heart bid goodbye to all at home including his brave female Jane and reported within three days.

The Indian army was placed on maximum alert. Army units were moved to forward positions along the international border and at LOC in Jammu and Kashmir. Indian Air Force was also placed on high alert. At least five train load of men and equipments had already arrived along with the division of Major Aditya Singh.

The Indian Army's movements came after report that Pakistan's army had moved some of its formations to forward areas. Two Pakistani air force fighters intruded with Indian Space in Jammu and Kashmir. Now the war was inevitable, Indian Armed Forces were ordered to retaliate the way they feel right. All the political parties supported the move and stand taken by Indian Prime Minister.

Aditya was leading the JAT REGIMENT to counter Pakistan Army at Kargil Sector. They (Pakistanis) were in Advantageous position to cover Indian Army. They were firing heavy artillery on Indian Army. They were on higher level.

Twenty five Pakistani soldiers were killed before fourteen Indian troops from Jat regiment and parachute commandos laid down their lives on the North Western slopes of the position at a height of 16000 feet after seven hours of intense fighting. Aditya was now the commanding officer for this troop and also the troops from Jammu and Kashmir Infantry. The Pakistanis were well entrenched and had made a number of field fortifications. Since the infiltrators had covered most of the approaches by fire, the Indian troops led by Aditya, in the face of intense shooting and heavy odds, scaled the objective and reached the top employing specialized mountaineering techniques. Aditya with his team approached the quaid post from an unexpected direction, using a longer and more different approach. After reaching the top, he lobbed a grenade into the bunker and closed the door, killing all Pakistani soldiers inside. Then the two sides got involved in hand to hand combat in which the Indian Soldiers bayoneted some of the Pakistani soldiers outside the bunker. Aditya was seriously injured, wounded but showing exemplary courage, he picked up the light machine gun and charged at the Pakistanis killing four of them. Later major Aditya succumbled to injuries. Aditya and his team made a supreme sacrifice in the traditions of the Indian Army and it was because of the gallant soldiers, the recapture of this vital position was made possible.

Aditya lost his life but won the Kargil conflict. He was wrapped in Tricolour and was brought to Mathura, his native place with complete national respect. For Aditya the bereavement stated with a knock at the door. The news came in a person by a military chaplain and a service member. They arrived in full uniform, bearing the worst news. This was the visit Jane never wanted. Aditya's remains (body) was packed in ice inside aluminium, flag-draped "transfer case". Mortal remains of Major Aditya Singh who died in the line of duty was consigned to flames with full military honours.

The moment, Jane saw that coffin, covered by Indian flag brought by Indian Army, she fainted. The entire country cried for him along with Jane. There was a very thin line between courage and supreme sacrifice. She had already sunk into the depth of depression and defeatism. The words spoken by Karan Veer to Jane, were very compassionate and nurturing of all times.

He said to Jane, "BETA, we have lost one Aditya for the country and for the honour of all of us so that we can keep our heads held high. We have two Adityas to grow." You are my very courageous and igneous daughter now.

Aditya was rest in peace with full military honours and he became an icon for all the youngsters for years to come.

CHAPTER – 41

After the Inevitable

There were numerous soldiers and officers who never returned to the comfort of their homes, to the warm hugs of their wives and children. This is the moment every army wife dreads.

Though people did uphold her status as a martyr's wife but army didn't take care of her financially. When Jane looked into eyes of her children, she only saw a void which she would never be able to fill in her life time. She knew that she would never be loved again like she was loved. Knowing all this, she was left with no alternative but to don the role of the head of family. She remembered the day to hear the tragic news that her husband had laid down his life for the nation. The officials were kind enough and empathetic when I opened the door, I saw a large number of people.

"I learned a lot from Aditya and today, I feel that my entire energy came from him. Two weeks before his death, he mailed me which I read every day. He told me to be strong, be solid, live life and love it. Don't grieve too long as I will always remain around you."

My seven years old sons had a tough time and were telling me how much they missed him. I see his pictures, his clothes in the cupboard and I all the time feel that he is on his way home. Aditya was a god husband and a good father. Yes, Aditya is gone forever and all our lives are changing. Aditya always gave me the experience of being loved from moment to moment, the affection, the tenderness, the words lover use, the listening the sensibility, the respect, willingness to participate in all relationship.

He had completed many things like making of WILL, meeting all relations and clearing all the debts etc, making LIC Policies for DEV and VED. I now think that he had the PREMONITION of death that is why he wanted to do too many things too early. Today also I feel, when close my eyes, I feel that he is touching me, holding my hand protectively on roads, malls, theatres, stoking my hair and kissing me all over. Jane expressed with grief that if she was given another chance to choose she would not hesitate to choose a soldier as her life partner. God was kind that I married that olive green and that was indeed a privilege to have married Aditya. She would live quiet with dignity and grace of an army officer's wife.

Salma today cried like a Rudaali for her brother.

Aditya was Aditya, Aditya is Aditya. Yes, Aditya was born different and he was special.

CHAPTER – 42

Jane retires

Time took a huge leap. Jane was wathching both her sons DEV & VED in olive green uniform as young Lieutenants. She was enjoying the images of Aditya in her two sons.

She retired from her job. She joined two NGOs which were working one for eradication of Rudaali system and other for welfare of war widows.

Now Jane was born different. She was special.

Little write up on Paragraph of earlier published three books;

1st - LOVE ON VENTILATOR

Ajit never felt insulted as he understood the mental agony and turmoil of Sudha. He will never leave Sudha with a broken heart and hope. He was not to satisfy his adrenaline rush as he had a firm belief that desire as a reason for mating is the way of animals.

2nd - LOVE TRIOLOGY WHO TO COMPLAIN

She was not responding to people and surrounding activities. The doctor arrived and after examination turned this as COMA or COMATOSE. He advised Ajit to treat it as medical emergency.

3rd - IT'S OK TO FALL IN LOVE AGAIN

She also knew that a single woman, both at home, college or at work, has to face many advances from men young and old, married and unmarried.

To be single and specially an unwed mother is taken as that she is available or easy to gain access to.

Printed in the United States
By Bookmasters